ICE LORD'S FATE

Bride of the Fae, Book 2

Ava Ross

ICE LORD'S FATE

Bride of the Fae, Book 2

Copyright © 2022 Ava Ross

All rights reserved.

No part of this book may be reproduced in any form or by any electronic or mechanical means, including information storage and retrieval systems, without written permission from the author, except for the use of brief quotations with prior approval. Names, characters, events, and incidents are a product of the author's imagination. Any resemblance to an actual person, living or dead is entirely coincidental.

Cover by The Book Brander

Editing/Proofreading by JA Wren & Owl Eyes Proofs & Edits

 Created with Vellum

Foreword

A note to the reader.

If you found this book outside of Amazon,
it's likely a stolen/pirated copy.
Authors make nothing when books are pirated.
If authors are not paid for their work,
they can't afford to keep writing.

*For my mom who
always believed in me.*

Series by AVA

Mail-Order Brides of Crakair

Brides of Driegon

Fated Mates of the Ferlaern Warriors

Fated Mates of the Xilan Warriors

Holiday with a Cu'zod Warrior

Galaxy Games

*Alien Warrior Abandoned/
Shattered Galaxies*

Beastly Alien Boss

Bride of the Fae

Screamer Woods
Orc Me Baby One More Time

Stranded With an Alien
Frost

You can find my books on Amazon.

Ice Lord's Fate

**Elion is mine,
and I won't let anyone steal him away.**

Elion and I have escaped the evil encroaching on the castle and fled to Elion's ice-covered estate. We're finally together, but the peace we find in his childhood home is short-lived. We spend our days working with friends to restore the true king to the throne, something his son and an evil witch refuse to see happen, and our nights clinging to each other.

And the clock is ticking.

Unless I can end Elion's curse, he'll die. In desperation, I search the kingdom, determined to break the witch's curse before it steals him from me forever. I refuse to lose him. He's my life and my love, and I'll lay down my life to save his.

But what if my sacrifice isn't enough?

Ice Lord's Fate is book two in a fantasy romance duology. This series heats to a high sizzle and comes with a guaranteed happily ever after.

Warning: Don't read this book unless you're open to steamy romance, mystery & danger, and you're intrigued by the idea of becoming a bride to a fae ice lord.

Prologue
RAVEN

"Wife," Elion said with intense satisfaction. He cupped my face and kissed me before lifting his head.

"Husband," I said, solely because I could. I laughed, and while the sound was a bit giddy, I didn't care. I loved him, and we were finally together.

Nothing was going to come between us.

He took my hand and pressed my palm against his chest. "Do you feel my heart beating? It does so for you and you alone. You are my fated mate, the only one I will ever love."

"Elion." I grinned and took his hand, pressing it against my chest. "Do you feel my heart? It's yours for now and always."

"Raven." His smile faded, replaced with stark reverence on his face. "I want you."

"Then take me."

He swept me off my feet and cradled me in his arms,

striding from the gorgeous chapel and outside. Despite the icy ground, he never faltered. He carried me inside the small castle, Koko scampering at his heels, and kicked the front door shut behind us. Turning, he started up the broad staircase.

"You're going to be worn out before we reach wherever we're going," I said with a chuckle. He made carrying me seem effortless with his even breathing and his heart thrumming at the same rate as it had in the chapel.

"Never," he vowed. At the first-floor landing, he strode across a balcony and around, carrying me up the second flight of stairs without stopping.

"I hope there aren't twelve floors," I said, unable to stop grinning. I was no skinny thing, and I'd never thought a guy would be able to do more than stumble across the threshold with me in his arms.

"Three floors," he said. "We're going to my suite."

"*Your* suite, huh?" I pictured what a young lord's room must look like. Toys long abandoned. Dirty underwear still lying on a chair. But that was a human teenage guy's room, not something I'd find in a castle. "Do you have posters of your favorite rock stars hanging on the wall?"

He frowned. "How can a rock be a star?"

"It's complicated. That's a no to posters, then."

"You are correct." He strode up the last flight of stairs. A broad balcony waited at the top with sofas and pretty tables placed in cozy sitting areas. Big urns with dried flowers stood here and there to give the place an elegant yet welcoming feel.

He crossed the balcony and strode down a long hall with only two doors on the right side. "This wing houses my suite."

"I have a feeling I'm not going to find a twin bed with Mickey Mouse sheets in your bedroom."

His smile widened. "I believe you know what you're going to discover in my bedroom, love."

A thrill shot through me. I wanted to take his hand and run through deep grass with butterflies soaring around us. To lay on any handy surface and tug him down on top of me.

I couldn't wait to feel the thrill of his touch.

He nudged open the second door on the right and carried me inside the room. Koko scampered in behind us. He circled the room, sniffing everything.

A big bed jutted out prominently from the right wall, with a door beyond. Floor to ceiling windows covered the front wall. I bet I could stand near them and look out at the back lawn.

"There is ice everywhere," he grumbled. "I'm sorry."

He was right. The entire place was encrusted, and sadness threatened to drag down my cheery mood.

Nothing could truly ruin this moment between us, but my heart pinched for Elion. He must want to show me the best parts of his home, but instead, the witch had frozen everything he loved.

"We can warm it up," I said, gesturing to the fireplace.

"Our love warms me through."

He said the sweetest things.

"But I will not see you shivering." He lowered me to my feet and lifted his arms. A soft, light blue mist drifted off his fingers. It swept through the room like a summer breeze, and everywhere it touched, the surface melted until only a cozy bedroom remained.

He nodded to the bed. "We need sheets and blankets, but I will take care of that."

A closet on this side of the bed gave us everything we needed, also warmed by Elion's magic. I helped him make the bed, eager to tumble between the silky sheets with him.

Husband. I pretty much breathed the word and was tempted to pinch myself to make sure I wasn't dreaming.

Had I imagined us getting married?

Rounding the bed, he swept open the door on the other side, revealing an enormous bathroom complete with a tub the size of a small pool.

Magic soon had the faucet filling the oval tub with steaming water.

"Would you like to join me in a bath, my love?" he asked, leaning against the doorframe. His hand rose to the top button of his billowy white shirt, and he tugged it through the hole, revealing skin I ached to touch. Kiss. Lick if he let me.

I had a feeling he would.

I undressed and sauntered toward him. His eyelids hooded, and he muffled a groan.

Shutting Koko out of the bathroom, we climbed into

the tub, him settling on a seat with me straddling his lap. His skin felt amazing against mine. I couldn't stop rubbing, eager to feel every bit of him pressed against me. Inside me.

It wasn't long before we were kissing and stroking each other. A fever grew within me, and only he was my cure.

He leaned forward and sucked my nipple into his mouth. When his tongue glided across it, I moaned and arched my spine, giving him complete access to my body. I was on fire for him, and nothing would make me happier than to feel him buried inside me. But this moment was more than about making love.

I needed that complete feeling I only found within his arms.

I rocked against him, pressing myself against his hard, thick length.

His fingers stroked my clit while he continued to deliver pleasure to my breast.

I jerked forward as everything inside me started to spiral.

He must've sensed how close I was because he lifted me and centered the tip of his cock against my core.

With his eyes locked on mine, he lowered me onto him until I'd taken all of him inside me.

"Elion," I gasped.

"Tell me what you need, love."

"Everything. I'm greedy. Give it to me."

His lips twitched upward. "I'll give you all I have, and then give myself to you all over again."

"Take me. Make me feel." I needed him to love me so completely that I could forget, even if it was only for one precious moment, that the witch was determined to steal him from me forever.

"Raven," he growled. He turned me to face away from him. Holding me close, he lifted me up and when he brought me back down, he thrust upward. Somehow, the position worked, him driving himself inside while my body rushed down to encase his.

The water splashed, and our groans filled the room.

When I'd turned into a gasping, moaning wreck, unsure I could take any more before blasting into a thousand pieces, he lifted me and laid me on the tub surround with him behind me.

He spread my legs wide and drove himself inside.

That was all it took. My mind shot to the clouds and kept going, blasting all the way past the stars.

He followed, holding me close, his body enfolding mine.

We found completion together.

Chapter 1
Raven

A scraping sound woke me, and I sat up in bed, my heart thrumming in my ears.

Elion slept beside me; his body relaxed. Something twisted inside me when I caught the expression of pure satisfaction on his face.

I'd put that look there when I gave him the gift of my heart and my body. Nothing would make me happier than to do so every day for the rest of my life.

But what had I heard? I searched the dark room with wide eyes but didn't see anything worth investigating.

Moonlight filtered through the ice-encrusted windows lining the right wall, casting shadows on the furniture placed here and there inside the enormous bedroom. If I let myself, I could be easily overwhelmed by all this. I was living in a freakin' castle!

Seeing the shy excitement on Elion's face after he'd warmed our room made me eager to gush. It wasn't hard. This place, even encrusted with ice, was gorgeous. And his bedroom had to be the nicest suite in the place. My apartment back home could fit inside with room left over for more.

When the scraping sound wasn't repeated, I laid back down, snuggling beneath the blankets while stealing the warmth from Elion he so eagerly gave. He mumbled, and his arms coiled around me, tugging me into his heady embrace.

I wanted so much for us.

Being together was a given.

Breaking his curse was my top priority, of course.

I wanted the chance to see our love grow and deepen.

I clung to the hope that if I loved him enough, I could help him. There had to be a way.

We had less than two weeks to break his curse. The thought crashed through me like a truck going ninety miles an hour hitting a stone wall. My mouth went dry, and tears stung the back of my eyes. I sniffed. It wasn't enough time. That damn witch. She'd changed the rules.

She wanted my Elion dead.

A scratching sound reached me from outside. Was a branch scraping across the siding? Maybe a random creature was racing along the outer sill. Were there squirrels in the fae kingdom?

When the curse was laid on Elion, his world froze solid. Everything had been locked in place at that exact moment, including any potential squirrels.

Elion would create what we needed with magic, just like he had the meal we'd eaten after we'd satisfied our hunger for each other. But everything else would remain locked as it was until the spell was broken.

Koko blinked up at me from where he'd coiled into a fluffy ball at the foot of the bed.

When the scratching sound was repeated, his head snapped around, and he peered toward the window. He bared his little teeth and hissed.

I gulped. Should I wake Elion? He was tired. Using magic to warm our room and bring us food had drained him.

The curse drained him.

Waking him for something as silly as this felt cruel.

It was a stick. A bit of tile dropping off the roof. It was *nothing*.

I flopped onto the bed, but I couldn't get back to sleep.

"All right," I whispered. "Go look at the branch, and *then* you can ignore the sound." I slipped from our bed, shivering when my bare feet touched the floor, and grabbed a wrap from a chair, swirling it around my body to help hold in the heat.

I crossed the room on tiptoe to look out the window.

Something moved across the back lawn, a shadowy being whose feet didn't touch the ground. Long hair flowed out behind her.

I leaned forward, pressing my nose against the glass, trying to figure out who it might be.

Betts? She and Nuvian left the king's castle together to come here. Nuvian wanted to find a way to break the curse and redeem himself in Elion's eyes. Betts . . . crushed on Nuvian, and she'd gone with him.

Elion and I planned to search for them in the morning.

Dense woods, the trees so leaden with ice that the tips of their upper branches nearly touched the ground, marched from the cliffs beyond down to the back lawn.

The ghostly figure bolted toward the woods, the hem of her dark gown fluttering in the wind. A creature unlike anything I'd seen before trotted beside her. A big dog?

My swallow went down hard.

A hyena the size of a pony sniffed the ground before tipping its head back and releasing a stuttered growl. The woman paused, and the beast caught up to her.

I didn't dare breathe. I remained as frozen as this castle, watching through the window.

When she reached the edge of the lawn, she lifted one hand. A path opened in front of her, slicing through the forest. She stepped toward it, but before her feet hit the trail, she turned back.

The woman in the dining room portrait—the one whose eyes seemed to watch me—looked toward Elion's home.

Now I remembered where I'd seen her before. This was the witch, the one who'd changed from a bird into an evil old woman. She'd tried to kill us the day we rode glisteers with the other human women in the forest.

This evil being had cursed Elion.

Her gaze raked up the tall stone building until it

locked on the window where I stood. Hatred flashed red in her eyes.

With a gulp, I flung myself to the side, hiding behind the wall between the windows, shaking like never before. Despite the chill in the air, a bead of sweat hitched down my spine, spreading shivers through me like hoarfrost etching across glass.

Being naked with Elion was the most wonderful thing in the world. Standing in a chilly room while someone watched me? Not so much.

I tossed the blanket aside and tugged my gown over my head, stuffing my feet into my sandals. They were totally impractical footwear, but I was wearing them when we left the king's castle. With quakes tracking down my spine, I wrapped the blanket around my body again, though nothing was going to warm me now.

I didn't have magic. I knew very little about this world I'd married into. But one thing was clear.

The witch who'd cursed the man I loved knew we were together. I bet she knew we'd married.

I counted to ten, then peeked through the glass again.

She still watched.

This time, when she caught my eye, she lifted her bony finger, pointing it at me. A murky yellow mist shot from the tip, blasting against the glass.

A bit of it made its way inside, and it sought me.

Found me.

Engulfed me.

The air around me shimmered.

In a blink, I stood in a mist-filled world made up of

dark clouds and fury. While I couldn't see it, I felt the world churning around me.

I turned, my hands reaching out for anything to grab onto, but finding nothing but air and white mist. Even my feet were planted in a gray-streaked cloud.

Where was I?

Panic roared through me, and I struggled to keep it from grabbing onto me and bolting.

"Elion?" I whimpered. My teeth chattered, and my skin went clammy.

Something shrieked to my left, and I faced that direction with only my stupid human hands lifted to protect me.

Footsteps thundered my way, and a beast unlike anything I'd seen before emerged from the smoke. It was a pony. No, a big dog. A magical mix of a wolf and a saber-toothed tiger.

When it saw me, it shrieked again. It rushed toward me, its long tusks slashing through the air.

Chapter 2
Elion

I woke when a chill swept through the room and found Raven gone from my side.

"Love?" I called out, but she didn't reply.

Koko scrambled onto my chest, his tiny claws digging into my skin. He stopped near my face with horror and fear blazing in his eyes.

Raven.

I shifted him to the side and leaped from the bed, my head snapping in all directions, seeking my wife. My love. The only woman I'd ever crave. "Raven?"

She was not in the room.

I also found the bathroom empty, plus the sitting room on the opposite side of the bath.

After wrenching on pants and stuffing my head and arms through my billowy white shirt, I ran to the door and wrenched it open, bracing my palms on the frame.

"Raven?" I bellowed, but only the empty hall replied

with a morbid echo. *Raven, Raven, Raven.* It mocked me like the witch had when she cursed me.

Koko leaped off the bed and ran over to stand beside me. He whimpered and jerked his head toward the windows.

I bolted over to them, stuffing my feet into my boots as I passed.

At the window, I spied Maverna standing near the woods.

When she saw me, she smirked. Dank yellow mist clouded around her, coating her.

Why had she cursed me? I still had no answer.

But hope had bloomed within me when I found Raven. I loved her, and surely a love as powerful as ours could break a curse laid on me in spite.

Maverna waggled her finger at me, and I lifted a magical block to stop whatever spell she sent my way.

She scowled, but I could tell her heart wasn't in it, because she didn't try again.

I knew why she didn't bother. She'd accomplished her mission already.

With her minion by her side, she turned and sauntered into the forest, taking a path I'd never seen before. The woods snapped back into place the moment she'd passed, leaving no trail to follow.

"She stole Raven," I whispered.

Koko whimpered again and oddly held up a paw.

"Where is she?" I cried, my heart bursting with terror. I had to find her and save her. "Did Maverna take her?"

Koko shook his head. Was I foolish to waste time quizzing a resha? The pet had bonded with Raven. He loved her. And all knew reshas would do anything for the one they loved.

I stooped down and held my hand out to Koko. "Can you find her? No, take me to her?"

Koko laid his paw on my palm, and magic unlike anything I'd felt before blasted across me, a tsunami headed for shore on a path of pure destruction. But I sensed no malice in this magic, only pure love, as if the two forces had long since combined into one that couldn't be beaten.

I had no time to analyze what this might mean.

Smoke choked my throat, and the misty world of the inner realm surrounded me.

Raven must be here.

Of course. Maverna dumped her in this horrifying location. She'd warned me to stay away from the woman I loved. She'd told me she'd do everything to stop us.

She knew Raven could be the key to breaking the curse, and there wasn't anything she wouldn't do—include mete out death—to make sure Raven didn't help me.

Despair dropped through me, making me shudder. I was nearly helpless in the inner realm, and Maverna knew it. I'd barely begun to practice traveling through the realm, but more often than not, I wound up in the wrong place rather than where I'd aimed to be.

Smoke clogged my lungs, and it was all I could do to remain on my feet.

I shored myself up with the love I carried for my wife.

"Raven," I called, then louder. "Raven!" I possessed strong magic. It would take me to her. My will alone would ensure that happened.

Koko leaned against my side, maintaining contact. Fur bristled along his back, and he peeled back his lips, revealing tiny, sharp teeth. He hissed, his snout pointing to our right.

"Find her," I commanded, my hand lifted. Magic swirled away from me, seeking, and I wasn't surprised when it snapped back, telling me to go right.

I lifted her tiny, precious pet and ran in that direction, my footsteps nearly silent on the moss-covered, cloudy ground.

Something growled far ahead. Thuds rang out, followed by the shriek of a hunter stalking prey.

Koko flung himself from my arms and raced in that direction.

Raven screamed, the sound ripping across my skin like barbed wire.

Chapter 3
Raven

Something out of a nightmare ran toward me.

Almost effortlessly and without more than a thought, claws extended where my nails used to be. But unlike the other times this frightening aberration had come to my defense, I felt something else inside me shift sideways. There was no other way to describe it.

Something was revealed. It coiled within me, watching.

The beast emerged from the mist, a creature from a nightmare made up of muscle, gnashing teeth, and slashing horns. It would soon tower over me—kill me—but I couldn't seem to make my body turn and run.

Fear ratcheted up my spine, and I broke out in a cold sweat. My hair spiraled around me, and lights bloomed within the clouds beneath my feet.

The lights came from me.

How was this possible?

"Stop," I said, my voice coming out calm, deep, and

deadly all at once. How could this low, guttural, yet magical sound come from within me?

The beast rushed toward me, its claws raking through the misty ground. It should fall through the gaps, yet it found purchase, its glowing red eyes locked on me.

"Approach me at your own risk," I said.

Yeah, leave it to me to suddenly act like I was starring in a fantasy movie.

Why in the world was I talking in a firm, commanding tone when I should be bolting in the other direction?

I caught a blur on my left, something tiny emerging from the mist. I crouched, expecting yet another beast to storm from that direction.

Instead, Koko hurtled toward me, his bushy tail spiked high, his little teeth gnashing.

"Sweetie," I said as he flung himself between me in the beast. I scooped him up, holding him tight.

How had he gotten here?

Elion.

"Elion!" I shrieked. He shouldn't be here. The thing stalking me would hurt him.

Koko's fur bristled as the saber-wolf stalked toward me, each step of its paws a death knell for us both.

I couldn't fight it off. By the way he strained to break my hold, Koko would do everything, even sacrifice himself, to defend me. I couldn't let him do that.

I lowered him to the ground and rushed around him, toward the beast.

Another creature lurked in the mist beyond it. A griffin? As long as it didn't come close, I didn't care what it was right now.

"Go," I shouted to the first beast. "You have no place here!" This was stupid. Like I could keep this terrifying thing from hurting me or Koko with clichéd words alone?

The beast roared, towering over me, the slash of its tusks making wind smack my face. Spittle dripped from its snout and when it hit the clouds by my feet, it burned through them, revealing a dark blue sea churning far below.

I slashed out, raking my claws across its throat. They bit deeply, and the beast shrieked, tipping its head back. It curled its neck, screaming, and my own cries joined in, creating an unearthly cacophony that must echo throughout this strange and terrifying world.

Another gouge with my claws left long gashes in its front leg.

It boiled with fury, shrieking and stomping around me, somehow never touching.

"Go," I cried, my spine quivering with rage. "You are banished from this place forever."

The words felt projected from my soul.

The creature dropped to its paws, as limp as a sail in calm seas. It stared at me with its glowing eyes until the light behind them winked out.

A pop, and it disappeared, leaving me with nothing but the taint of brimstone clogging my sinuses and ash swirling through the air.

Koko whined beside me, and I lifted him, snuggling

him against my throat. Flames licked through my chest, trying to burn their way free.

My claws receded.

What the hell had just happened?

I wasn't magical, and I sure wasn't a fae. Whatever lurked inside me didn't come from my human mother.

"Who was my father?" I bellowed loudly enough to make Koko jump. He peered up at me, his eyes soft and somehow knowing.

"If only you could speak, little guy," I said, keeping my voice soft. "If only you could tell me who I am and what this means."

Steps behind me sent me whirling. A growl roared up my throat and a tingle shot down my fingers, telling me my claws were erupting again.

Elion appeared from the mist; his face cloaked in stark fear.

He gathered me in his arms, holding me as my claws once again receded.

Chapter 4
Elion

While I needed much more practice before traveling extensively within inner realm, I had mastered placing myself a few locations.

Calling magic, I swirled it around us.

A flash made me blink.

We should've stood in my bedroom again. Instead, we stood in a place I'd never traveled to before. Worse, I didn't recognize it.

"Where are we? It looks like a cave," Raven whispered, stepping out of my arms but keeping hold of my hand.

When Koko struggled, she lowered him to the dirt floor. He paced around the cave in widening circles before stopping beside what looked like the only exit from the room, a triangular-shaped opening that rose to about chest-height.

The cave was about thirty feet across, and the ceiling

had to be two stories above. Boulders networked the floor, and stone spikes dangled down from the roof. A dark-leafed vine entwined around the spears and draped across the upper walls, slowly weaving back and forth in a dance to an unheard tune. Tiny white flowers bloomed on the vine, releasing a sickly-sweet perfume into the air. It clogged my sinuses and made me want to sneeze.

Koko peered back at us from the exit and cheeped.

"Whoa," Raven said, clutching her head. "My head is spinning."

The flowers.

Fighting through the fog brought on by the scent, I pulled her back against my chest and summoned an enclosure spell, but the smell permeated my magical cloak. When Raven's knees started to give way, I lifted her off her feet, barely able to remain awake myself.

My gaze blurring, I staggered around the boulders, aiming for the triangular exit where Koko still waited, his tiny paws padding the soil in distress.

Stooped down, I hobbled into a dark passage with Koko at my side. I didn't slow until I tripped and nearly fell over something lying on the ground. At least by then, the scent had faded, and I'd regained my wits.

Koko leaned against my leg, releasing a soft whimper.

"Raven?" I whispered, tugging her close.

When she didn't reply, I cast a light spell, though I kept it muted. I didn't know where we were or why my magic had brought us to this location, but I sensed someone else's magic could be involved, and I didn't want to draw their attention.

Damn Maverna. I sensed her involvement here.

I wasn't going to make this easy for her. She'd only bring us here to kill us, and I refused to fall into her trap.

"Raven?" I murmured again. She slept, unconscious from the taint of the flowers, but she otherwise didn't appear to be in distress.

Koko watched her, his gaze full of sorrow.

Stiffening, he shot a scowl in the direction we'd come from. He whirled and hurried forward, taking a long passage that slowly sloped downhill, away from the cave, peering back to make sure I followed.

I kept pace with him, protecting Raven with my body curled around hers and the small bit of magic I dared use in this cursed place.

The tunnel bottomed out in a larger cave. I paused in the opening while Koko crept forward, stopping near a boulder to peer around the side.

I sent out magic, scanning the room, but nothing living lurked within the chamber. Before I dared to step into what could be another trap, I sent out a bit of magic, nothing larger than a bit of fluff floating in the air. It slowly coasted around the room, sending back information, though I didn't pick up much beyond multiple smooth, glassy sections interspersed in the outer walls and boulders strewn across the dirt floor.

Sending the fluff higher, I struggled to watch through the dander's "eyes," but this sort of magic wasn't easy. All I picked up were cloudy images of me standing in the opening holding Raven, Koko still hunched behind the boulder, and glossy panels lining the outer, circular wall of the room.

I sent more magic through the arched opening on the opposite side of the cave, catching glimpses of another passage before my spell winked out. Holding my breath, I waited to see if someone had caught me spying before letting my lungs deflate. If someone had dispelled my magic, they hadn't been obvious about it.

I remained where I was, unsure if I dared move forward when Koko still seemed uncertain.

"Raven?" I whispered in her ear.

She stirred, shifting in my arms, and her eyes opened. "Elion." Snuggling her face into my neck, she kissed me. A frown creased her brow, and she paused, a shudder wracking her frame. She peered around. "Where are we?" she whispered. "I remember flowers. They smelled awful."

"The cave we landed in was coated with vines cloaked in magic," I said softly. "As for where we are now, I'm not sure. I found you in the inner realm. "

"The misty world. The witch dragged me there."

I wouldn't say her name. "When I tried to take us back to my estate, we were brought here instead."

"Brought." Her lips curled down. "I'm sure this serves her purpose. When I was in the inner realm, as you called it, a horrible creature raced toward me, but I fought it off." She held up her hands. "Claws appeared on the tips of my fingers again." Her concerned gaze met mine. "We need to figure out what's going on with me. I'm glad to have a way to defend myself, but it's scary. I feel out of control of everything, especially myself."

"Not us."

A smile flickered across her face. "I'll always trust us." She swallowed. "We need to avoid whatever trap the witch is about to spring."

"You're right." I lowered her to her feet. I'd gladly hold her forever, but two hands to dispense magic would protect her more than one.

Taking her hands, I kissed her knuckles. "You're amazing, no matter what. I want you to know that."

Her hand trembled. "I'm human, or I thought I was, but now I wonder about my father."

I'd wondered too. "Fae?" It would make the most sense.

She shrugged. "Do any of the fae sprout claws?"

"Not that I've heard of."

"Yet you can shift into a wolf with claws."

"I've only shifted since I was cursed; the two seem to be wrapped together, though I don't know why."

"Maybe I'm part wolf, then," she said.

"Wolf shifters are scorned by the fae."

She watched my face. "What about you?"

"My wolf is a part of me now, and I've come to love it as much as the rest."

Her smile broke through. "I love you no matter who you are, Elion."

I wanted to kiss her so much, but we couldn't afford the distraction.

"If I'm part wolf, I'll embrace that side," she said. "I

just hope I learn to control whatever it is. I don't like that this part of me takes over whether I want it to or not."

Back at the king's castle, Erleene said it was too soon to reveal information about Raven, but what about now? "I know of someone who may be able to help."

"Then let's get out of here and find that person. Can you magically transport us there?"

"It takes great power to move through the inner realm. I've practiced, but my skills are limited." And I wouldn't endanger Raven by going there again. From the shriek, I suspected she'd fought off a flazire, one of Maverna's minions.

Next time, Maverna would send more than one.

"Should we look for the witch?" she asked. "I'd rather avoid her, but now might be the time to do something about your curse. She's the source. Killing her would be a wonderful place to start."

"She won't be easy to kill, or I would've done so already." And no one could definitively say killing her would end my curse. It wasn't worth the risk to find out.

She nodded. "Do we continue forward, into a possible trap?"

"We can't return to the cave with the vines."

"Then forward it is." She scooped up Koko, holding him snug in her arms.

I followed, hovering close to her for protection.

She peered around the boulder, and her gasp rang out. Horror filled her gaze. "Elion. They're . . ." Her ragged breathing echoed in the room. "I can't . . ."

Following her gaze, a chill sunk into my bones.

ICE LORD'S FATE

The glossy panels I'd spied with magic were cases embedded in the wall with stone slabs on the sides, locking them in place. Each case held someone locked in magical suspension.

Follen was entombed in the one to my right.

Chapter 5
Raven

"Betts," I hissed, pain arching through my chest. I ran to a glass panel on my left, but when I reached out to touch the surface, Koko galloped over and thrust himself between me and the panel, growling.

I snapped my hand back and picked him up, holding him close to my chest.

"I don't understand," I whispered. "Why . . .?" I just couldn't fathom this.

She stared forward blankly, her body posed with her hands clasped on her chest and her feet even, as if she lay in a casket.

"Are they dead?" I cried out.

Elion gathered me in his arms, but while I welcomed his comfort, nothing would take away the anger and horror blasting through me.

"I don't think so," he said.

"I think they're . . . frozen. Locked up magically. *She* did this. That witch." Despite my rage, I wouldn't speak her name. My mother once told me that names had power, and I wouldn't do anything to call *her* attention to us.

She must know we were here because she'd sucked us into this trap.

"She wanted us to see them, to realize they're hopeless and so are we," I said. Holding Koko close, I strode around the room with tears stinging my eyes, taking in our friends locked motionless within each glass-covered chamber.

Betts. Nuvian. Follen.

And the king.

Others had been entombed with them, though I didn't recognize their faces. Elion did, though. I could see it in the stark pain filling his eyes as he stopped in front of each one.

"We have to free them," I whispered.

Koko squirmed, and I put him down. He trotted across the room and put his tiny paws up on the wall beneath the king. His soft whimper echoed around us.

"I'll try." Elion lifted his hands and closed his eyes. Magic shot from his fingers, but it ricocheted off the glossy surface of King Khaidill's case, diffusing when it hit the ceiling. The king stared forward, his eyes wide and his mouth ajar in horror.

They'd been frozen like Elion's castle and the world around it, the witch's calling card.

"Do you think this is part of your estate?" I asked.

Elion shrugged. He tried again, shooting magic at the area around the case holding Nuvian, but the rock absorbed the power, glowing before fading back to the dark gray stone it was before.

"How long before she arrives to do this to us?" I asked, backing toward the tunnel. "We need to get out of here."

"I'm going after her," he said, gesturing to the archway on the other side of the room. "I won't let her do this to anyone else. It ends now."

I grabbed his arm. "She's already stolen everything from you. Don't anger her, or she'll kill you outright."

"Listen to the girl," someone said in a sly voice from behind us.

Elion growled and blasted magic that way.

I spun, glaring at Maverna.

His power hit her, but it slid around her, soaking into the wall while causing her no discernable damage.

A lift of her hand, and Elion froze, his hands limp at his sides and his gaze locked forward.

Shit. It was over already. Panic exploded inside me. I had to run, but where could I hide?

She strode right up to me. "You, pitiful human, are clever." Frowning, she studied me from the top of my head to my toes. "Why can I not determine what you are?" Her head tilted. "Oh, wait. You're . . ." Surprise overtook her confusion. "No . . . It isn't possible." She cackled. "How wonderful if it was true, because . . ."

"I'm me. My mother's daughter and my sister's protector. I protect Elion too." I slashed out, raking my claws across her chest.

She gulped and looked down, horror dawning on her

face as blood welled in the wounds. "That is not possible. You cannot harm me. I've cast spells—"

"Release Elion or your throat is next."

She lifted a finger, and I flew backward, smacking into the stone wall.

Koko yelped and raced toward her, but she froze him in place.

Stars spiraled in the periphery of my vision. Shuddering, I slipped down the glossy surface, crumpling in a heap on the dirt floor.

Pain wracked my body, and for a second, I wasn't sure I'd be able to remain awake, let alone stand. But when Maverna's mocking laugh echoed in the cave, I couldn't do anything but get up. I spied a rock the size of my fist lying nearby and grabbed it.

"Would you like to join your friends, Ice Lord?" Maverna asked, standing near Elion. "It will be much easier to keep track of you if I turn you into another jewel in my magnificent display."

I rocked onto my knees and sucked in a deep breath, using my exhale to shove away the agony coursing through me.

Maverna lifted Elion. With a flick of her finger, she shot him toward a section of blank wall.

He oozed through the rocky surface with Koko. A blink and they hovered inside a case like the others. Elion stared forward blankly, his lips parted.

I screamed a tortured, wretched sound. This couldn't be happening.

Rage consumed me. I might be a weak little human,

but my heart was strong. I loved Elion and even death wouldn't keep me from saving him.

I staggered to my feet and raced toward Maverna.

She'd already dismissed me, and that would be her downfall.

I plunged the rock down hard on her head.

Turning, she gaped at me. Her hand rose, shaking, and she stared down at it with a frown.

I slashed out with my claws again, ripping through her throat, leaving gaping wounds that would kill anyone.

A pop, and she disappeared.

I dropped to my knees and cupped my face in my palms. Elion. Elion! Rising, I raced to the wall but no matter how hard I smacked the rock against the surface, the glass remained smooth and unmarred.

"Would you like to help Elion?" someone said from the archway on the right side of the room.

I spun, lifting my rock again, but my arm dropped when Erleene strode into the room.

She scowled at my friends—my love, Elion—locked within the walls. "She's at it again, is she?"

"I hit her hard. Sliced open her throat," I said with a sob. "She must be dead. Why didn't her spell end with that?"

"Sadly, she has probably repaired her throat already. She won't die that easily."

I turned to the wall holding Elion and Koko, but when I started to press my palm against the glass surface, Erleene held me back with magic.

"Do not do this unless you wish to join them," she said.

Maybe I did. Without Elion, I couldn't go on.

"I don't care. I'd rather be inside with him than lost without him out here." I whirled to face her. "She shortened his curse. He has less than two weeks left."

"Then we must work quickly."

"*We?* What do you expect me to do?" I cried with despair. I felt so helpless. Hopeless. If wanting to end his curse was enough, it would be gone already.

"First, you will release them from Maverna's cages," she said. "And then I will transport all of us to the elf kingdom."

"Let me find a bigger rock." If I hit it hard enough, I'd bash the glass and free them.

"Oh, no," she said, grabbing my arm as I passed. "That will not work."

"How do you expect *me* to free them?"

She gave me a smile I couldn't interpret. If I didn't know better, I'd think she was filled with excitement, not the horror churning through me.

"I will teach you the correct spell, *niece*."

Chapter 6
Elion

I dreamed.

A baby cried, and a woman soothed it, her fingers warm on his brow.

"Now, now, love," she whispered. "Hush. All will be well."

Thunder rumbled overhead and lightning flashed across the sky outside the window, bringing daylight to the dark room for only a few seconds.

It was long enough to see a beautiful fae woman with long, dark hair streaked with silver, leaning against colorful pillows in a satin-draped bed. I didn't catch her face, but I sensed I knew her.

A series of flashes outlined the room, and each revealed another piece of the big puzzle. An infant lying on her lap, swaddled in a blue velvet blanket. He slept; his tiny lips parted.

Someone bustled near the bed, another female ripe

with her own child. But with the light fading, I couldn't identify her. A maiden helping the first? Perhaps a sister or friend. Or a witch. They often assisted during childbirth.

"He is precious," the woman beside the bed said.

"Yes, isn't he? His father will be very pleased."

"When will you leave to take your son to him?"

"Soon. I must rest." Her voice faded. "I didn't expect to deliver early or I'd be there already. The birth was nearly too much for me." I sensed more than saw her tip her head back against the pillows, her eyelids fluttering. "I'm so tired..."

"Yes, yes, I put something in our broth to... help you rest." The other woman leaned over the baby. She glided her fingertips across his brow. "Sleep. I will watch over you both."

In a flash, I stood within the inner realm, heavy clouds choking around me.

I pulled magic and encased myself in a cloak spell, but no matter how hard I tried to send myself to a better place, I remained in this cursed inner world.

Howls rang out nearby, but that was nothing new. They sensed my arrival. They hunted me.

The fae were allowed to travel here, but it was unwise to remain long. This was a stopping point, a hub of sorts. A person arrived from one location and, with the right spell, transported themselves to another.

No one ever lingered. If they did so, the beasts would find them. A few who'd come here had never been seen again.

"You should have scorned her," someone said, striding over to stand beside me.

"Camile Du'patrice," I snarled. "I thought the king's guards had caught you. You should be dead by now for threatening Raven's life."

Her low chuckle rang out, echoing around us. She stroked her long blonde hair shot through with silver, her gown brushing across her golden sandals.

"His guard are not strong enough to entrap me," she said. "I carry the same blood as my sister."

"And who might that be?"

The conniving expression on her face bit through my confidence, making me waver. "Surely you already know."

"Maverna." I said it with certainty but watched her eyes.

They shifted away from mine. "Correct."

"You tried to kill my love. My mate. My Raven."

"And yet she still lives." She frowned. "I'm not sure why she has been able to escape our spells, but my sister and I will soon find out."

Movement beyond her drew my eye. A griffin? When I looked harder, though, I saw nothing.

"Stay away from Raven." I rushed Camile, grabbing her neck. Fury blasted through me. I would end this now.

A hitch of her arm was followed by a burning in my gut.

I gaped down at the blade sticking out of me, buried to the hilt.

"Try to evade *that*, Ice Lord," she said with a cackle.

A flick of her finger, and she melted, disappearing into the mist.

I staggered. Dropped to my knees. Gripping the hilt of the blade, I wrenched it out. Dark smoke billowed from the hole. It stank like something rotten consumed me. She'd cast a spell on it. This was not a normal wound.

The blade slipped from my fingers, dropping away, dissolving into the mist.

I gathered magic, tugging it in and, with my eyes closed, willed myself to be anywhere else. This was my last chance. If I didn't—

A thud, and I opened my eyes. I stood in my ice-encased library. Good, I'd escaped the realm. Yet . . .

Fog swirled through the room, dancing along the ice that covered everything.

I willed the ice to melt, but it remained firmly lodged in place.

Perhaps I wasn't inside my castle, but somewhere else?

"Elion," someone called, the pain in her voice shooting through me like an arrow. I fell to my knees again, and when I tried to rise, I couldn't find the strength to get up.

My belly wound continued to seep rot; the foul essence swirling around me. It would eat me from the inside out. So much for the time we thought we had left to break the curse. Camile had added another lethal layer.

I flopped forward, smacking on the hard floor. I panted, groaning with pain while the mist crept closer. It hovered around me, extending finger-like tendrils that nearly touched before snapping back into the churning mass.

Dragging myself toward the desk sitting in the right corner of the room, I tried to figure a way out of this situation. If the mist touched me, yet another layer of darkness would fall over me. I was certain of this.

"Elion," the voice called again. I knew her, but I couldn't place her. She was someone important. Precious.

Little human.

Raven.

"Raven," I cried. "Run. Don't come near me." I couldn't bear it if the mist surrounded her. It would slip inside her, change her, and she'd no longer be mine.

I reached the desk with the mist trailing behind me. It watched me. The moment I passed out, it would roar across me, and Raven would never be able to find me.

Grabbing onto the desk, I used it to pull myself up onto my knees, and then to my shaky feet. I staggered around the desk and collapsed in the chair behind it.

The mist coasted up over the desk, coming for me. Smoke coiled from the wound in my belly, meeting up with the mist. The two combined and formed an enormous snake. It coiled together on the hardwood floor, its head rising above the desk to hiss at me. A long tongue flicked out.

"Be gone," I snarled, flicking magic its way, but while my power sliced through it, it reformed and thickened, as if wounding it only made it stronger.

It stretched across the top of the desk but stopped

when it reached a scroll lying coiled up on the smooth wooden surface—the one I'd found in the king's castle and brought here. It spoke of a curse like mine, and I'd found one passage within it that gave me hope.

If a cursed fae can find love everlasting, and such a person was willing to sacrifice, almost any spell can be broken.

When I met Raven—my everlasting love—I'd found a reason to hold on. She was my true mate, the one I'd love throughout many lifetimes.

Could she break the curse? The scroll suggested it would take sacrifice, and I wouldn't trade myself for even one second that endangered Raven.

I snapped my hand out and grabbed the scroll, dragging it across the surface and clutching it to my chest.

The mist snake surged toward me with its fangs poised to bite.

I tried to stand, but sagged back into the chair, holding the scroll up like a talisman that would keep me safe.

But nothing would stop the mist beast from overtaking me.

Chapter 7
Raven

"*You're* going to teach me how to cast spells?" I asked Erleene, my eyes widening. "Not happening. I'm human, incapable of performing magic, remember?" Other than the claws that jolted from the tips of my fingers whenever I was in danger, I was completely normal. "Why are you taking this direction when Elion and our friends are trapped inside a wall?" Even Koko, the poor innocent resha. My eyes stung, and grief threatened to sweep me away. "We needed to rescue them before Maverna recovers from me ripping out her throat."

Hold on.

"Back up here a second," I said, swiping at my tears. "Did you just call me your *niece*?"

Erleene's smile brightened, and she held out her arms. "Welcome, little one. We are family."

Koko watched us from within the case—I swore it. His little face was creased with concern.

"Yeah, not so fast." I backed away until I ran into a boulder, then scurried around it, leaning to the side to watch her.

I swore I heard Koko snarl, though he remained unmoving. Yeah, he didn't trust Erleene any more than I did.

"You're *Follen's* sister," I said.

"I am." Her arms dropped to her sides, but her smile never wavered.

"How can you be my aunt?" Shit. "Are you saying Follen is my father? We don't look anything alike." Why I focused on his appearance was beyond me. Maybe I did it because my mind kept whirling, and my legs would barely support my weight. "He has pointy ears. Long white hair streaked with green. You and he are tall and willowy." Not short and—I could get away with "extra lush"—like me.

"Your father was our younger half-brother. We share elf blood."

"And what else?" This could give me some clue about my own identity.

"This and that." When she glanced away, I suspected she wasn't going to tell me what the other half of my father might be, but I assumed it was something that sprouted claws.

"You said *was*." Oh . . . "You mean he's dead." My eyes stung. It was all I could do not to sob.

Erleene's smile fell. "Yes. No."

"Which is it?"

"He is no longer with us."

I sagged against the boulder. My dad named me, then bailed on me and Mom, but I'd always hoped to meet him one day, even if all I did was snarl at him for abandoning us.

I'd thought maybe, just maybe, he had a reason for leaving us. He'd explain, we'd mourn Mom dying, and we'd get closer.

Since he was dead, I truly was an orphan.

"I hate to interrupt, as I can see you're flustered," Erleene said. "But—"

"Flustered?" Fists at my sides, I stormed out from behind the boulder. "Flustered?! I'm flustered, all right. No, I'm..."

I didn't know how I felt, but now wasn't the time to think about it.

"Forget me being related to you for the moment," I said, shoving my emotions to the side. "I need to help Elion and the others. Contrary to what you're suggesting, I don't have magical abilities. We don't have time for games. You need to break the glass holding him and the others inside the wall and get us out of here."

"We are dealing with two things here," she said, watching me. What did she see? Probably a woman who has had her world thrown into a blender and pureed. "My powers are limited when it comes to Maverna's spells. This is a sacrifice I made long ago to help another. I can transport us through the inner realm, but I cannot break her spell holding them inside the wall. Only you can do that."

"I keep telling you. I can't do magic," I shouted.

"But you can. It was suppressed, but I, fortunately, have the skill to unlock part of it." She held up her hand before I could speak. "The rest will come in due time. However, keep in mind that you're only part-elf. You will never be as powerful as one of full blood."

An elf. I felt the tops of my ears, but they remained as rounded as the last time I'd touched them.

I was pure Mom.

Erleene must be mistaken; we weren't related.

I wanted to pin her against a wall and make her answer the questions floundering around inside me, but time was running out. How long before Maverna recovered and returned to finish what she'd started? It wouldn't be long.

She'd be out for blood—mine.

"You realize this is a horrible time to spring this on me," I said. "Why didn't you tell me earlier?"

"Now is the correct time."

I didn't agree but I sensed arguing would get me nowhere.

"So, what do I have to do?" I asked, truly not believing I could make a difference, but willing to try anything.

"Draw your claws to the surface and rip Elion and the others from the wall."

"My claws only appear when I'm desperate," I said.

Her white eyebrows lifted. "Do you not feel desperate now?"

Anger and dismay churned through me. I *did* want to

rip something apart. Preferably, Maverna, but the glass encasing Elion would also do.

I stormed over to where he floated, staring forward, not seeing the pain burning me from the inside out.

Poor Koko's gaze followed me, and I sensed so much fear and sadness there.

Closing my eyes, I willed the claws to appear, but when I looked down, my fingertips remained the same.

"How do I do it?" I bellowed.

Erleene's hand dropped onto my shoulder. "Patience. Heartmagic like yours must come from deep within you. It must be pure and unfettered by emotion. It is a blade you can wield, one with great power, and I believe one day you will use it when you have the greatest need. However, lashing out with magic is never the way. Do not let anger or fear control your actions or the magic will control you."

Unable to bear seeing Elion suspended, I closed my eyes again, blocking out everything, even Erleene's touch.

I also shoved aside my excitement and dismay. She was my aunt? A part of me longed to step back against her, to seek her touch. She was family. I had my sister waiting back in the human realm, but I missed Mom and the guidance she provided.

Erleene could give that to me. She wasn't Mom, but she was a woman older than me with life experience.

I shoved my longing aside.

Deep within me, something smoldered, waiting, like the bit of a flame struggling to consume a candlewick.

Was this heartmagic? I gently blew on it, feeding it, and I sensed rather than felt heat floating off it.

Not sure why I did it, I scraped across the surface of the heat, bunching what little I could remove together in a small, writhing, molten ball.

Then I tossed it up into the sky, telling it to find its way out—through my fingers.

"Yes," Erleene breathed. Her fingers tightened on my shoulder. "Well done."

I held up my hands, admiring the lethal claws spiking from the tips. "I have no idea why these appear, but I'm glad to have them if they can help Elion and my friends."

I swore I saw pride in Koko's eyes.

"Free Elion," Erleene said, the urgency in her voice transmitting itself to me. "We don't have much time, and we need to release the rest of them or . . ."

"She'll kill them."

"Eventually."

I didn't want to think about the horror she implied. I had one focus, and it was time to complete something she said only I could do.

I slashed out at the glass encasing Elion and Koko, and my claws glided through what should be a hard surface as if it was water. It coalesced into a pale brown fog I sensed meant me no harm. It flowed down onto the floor, leaving Elion and Koko exposed.

Koko yipped and leaped to the ground, scurrying around behind me.

Elion fell forward, into my arms, and I held him, carefully lowering him onto the floor.

Something thudded onto the ground by the wall, but I didn't spare it a glance.

Elion clutched his belly with both hands, and he winced as if incredible pain consumed him.

Erleene gasped. "They didn't . . . *No.*"

I peeled his fingers away from his belly, revealing a gaping wound.

Chapter 8
Elion

"Elion, please," Raven cried, her hand softly stroking my brow.

I woke suddenly, lying across her lap. Erleene stood nearby, her brow furrowed with dismay, and Koko whimpered, padding my arm with his tiny paw.

"How dare she do this?" Erleene asked.

"Camile," I gulped out, surprised at how weak my voice sounded. "Met her in . . . inner realm. Magic."

"Heal him," Raven said, her hand fluttering above the wound. "Fix this!"

"I cannot do it here," Erleene said. "However, I will take him someplace safe. You must free the others before Maverna returns."

"I was in . . . wall," I said, frowning. It was hard to remember anything but the inner realm.

"I freed you," Raven said. She held up her hand, displaying her claws. "I'm . . . I don't really know what I am. Erleene said my dad was her and Follen's younger half-brother, but that can't be."

She was part-elf, then. That would explain some of this. I'd suspected she wasn't completely human, though never related to Erleene and Follen.

"Free the . . . others," I said, biting back the groan hurling itself up my throat. If I cried out, Maverna would hear me. Camile too. They'd come here, and it would be over. I knew this in my soul. "Leave me." I glared at Erleene. "Take Raven. Get her out of here."

"This is bigger than all of us, Ice Lord," Erleene said. "Bigger than Raven." Her gaze shot to the king. "So much bigger than you can imagine."

Koko scampered over to King Khaidill and sat beneath him, his soft cries echoing in the room.

"You have manipulated . . . others too long," I said. "Do. Not. Touch. Raven." My strength was waning fast. Soon, I'd pass out, and I suspected I'd never wake after that.

"She is mine," Erleene said. She shot Raven a look I couldn't define. "She is ours. She belongs to everyone. We need her."

"No, she belongs to . . . herself," I grated out. The wound was sucking my energy away. Soon, there would be nothing left of me but a husk.

"Raven has a purpose outside of being with you," Erleene said. "But she needs training. She won't get that from an ice lord husband."

"Leave her . . . alone." If only I could protect her from everyone who would hurt her. Erleene wouldn't purposefully cause my love harm and not only because they were related. But if Raven had to die, would Erleene stand in the way?

"If I free the others, will you heal him now?" Raven asked, her gaze remaining locked on mine. "I don't care about the other stuff. It means nothing! Only Elion matters."

Erleene grunted. "As I said, I cannot do it here. It'll take more than my power to reverse Camile's spell."

"Heal him," Raven snapped. Pain for me created grooves in her face. She stroked my forehead, taking care not to scrape me with her claws, and leaned close to speak in my ear. "I love you. I'll protect you. Nothing and no one will steal you away, not even death. You hear that? I'll follow you there and drag you back, so beware."

My rough laugh slipped out, making my chest and belly shake. The wound smoldered, eating me up, but I kept my face smooth. No matter what, I wouldn't show how much it hurt. I wouldn't frighten Raven.

Erleene watched us, and I sensed something else was at play here, though I couldn't imagine what it could be.

Nothing surprised me more than when she relented. "I will suspend her spell until it can be broken."

A sweep of her hand sent magic drifting over me. In seconds, the pain eased in my gut, and the smoke stopped coiling from my wound.

"Free them," Erleene said. "The king first."

Raven studied my face. "Are you okay?"

"I'm fine." I held back my wince. I could still feel the

poison working through me, but Erleene was right. We needed to get the king out of here.

"I don't like it; not any of this," Raven said, but she eased me onto the floor. She stepped around me, approaching the king with her claws extended. A few gouges through the surface, and the king fell forward.

Koko whimpered.

Erleene caught him, and Koko leaped onto the king's chest. A whoosh, and they both disappeared. Erleene glanced toward the far wall that shimmered, inky magic oozing through the stone, melting it. "Release the others. Hurry. She is coming."

Soon Nuvian, Bettina, and Follen were freed and spirited from here.

"We must leave," Erleene said, rushing toward us.

The wall shimmered, and a crack rang out as it split down the middle.

As Erleene swept me from the cave, Raven's hand slipped from mine.

"Raven," I cried as Erleene took me to safety, leaving my beloved behind to face the witch.

Chapter 9
Raven

I spun and bolted for the passage we'd used to arrive in the cave, but I didn't make it more than a few steps before something invisible swept over me. Like she'd wrapped a rope around my waist, Maverna yanked me backward.

I tumbled onto the ground, and she dragged me, hauling me closer until I lay on the dirt floor at her feet, staring up at her.

Camile stepped through the gap in the wall, joining Maverna.

"Kill her," Camile said. "We can end this now."

I scrambled to my feet, backing away from them.

They watched me like predators with matching smirks, and I wasn't sure why I hadn't guessed they were related already. It was in their faces and their similar coloring.

Maverna sighed. "You cannot run, puny human. My magic will find you wherever you may go." Her lips thinned as she took in the empty cases along the wall. "Who did this? Who stole my prizes?"

"I did." I took great pleasure in the surprise flashing on their faces. "You didn't think I had it in me, did you?"

Camile stormed toward me with her hands lifted. "Who are you? Why does so much rest on you?"

I expected to be blasted back against a boulder. I'd be crushed and would slump to the floor. It would be over. I'd never see Elion again, and I'd never get the chance to save him.

But when Camile shot something oily and misty toward me, it deflected off me.

I stared down, watching as her magic dropped to my feet and was sucked into the ground.

"Who are you?" Maverna cried out again.

"I'm me. Raven," I said with a lifted chin.

"There's something else about you, and we will figure it out," Camile said. She scowled at Maverna. "Kill her, and then you don't need to worry about her any longer."

"I would like to, but our magic doesn't appear to be doing what we want," Maverna said.

Frankly, if they wanted to stand around and fight about it, I'd let them. I inched toward a boulder. If nothing else, I could hide behind it.

Why had Camile's magic slid off me today when she was able to grab me by the throat that first day in the ballroom? And why was Maverna convinced there was something about me she needed to know?

Maybe there was something to what Erleene said. My father must play a role in this.

Speaking of Erleene, where was she? She should've come back for me already.

Unless she was afraid of facing Maverna and Camile together. This was speculation on my part, but if it was possible for her to reach me, I suspected she would. She wouldn't abandon me.

Nothing was clear in all this except I'd begun to believe she was right. I was part-elf, though I had no idea what I could do with my heritage.

Unsure of how to get away from Maverna and Camile, I opted to remain behind the boulder. Should I run back the way we'd come? They'd chase me, but maybe I'd find a place to hide.

"If we can't kill her," Camile said, "maybe we can lock her inside the wall. She freed the others, but I doubt she'll be able to free herself."

"We can't trust that will work," Maverna said. "If she gets free, she'll find a way back to him. She'll do what others believe she's capable of. She's determined and in the way. I'm not confident she won't find the path to our destruction."

"We could send her to the inner realm," Camile said. "I doubt she'll find her way free of that."

Yeah, I wasn't excited about returning there. I might as well risk the tunnel. Leaving my hiding spot behind the boulder, I tiptoed toward the dark opening.

"I placed her there, yet here she is," Maverna said.

"We could bury her," Camile said. "Fill in the cave and leave her here."

Maverna grunted. "That might work."

Camile yelped, and I felt her pointing my way. "We'll have to decide what to do with her before she escapes."

"Don't go anywhere, pesky human," Maverna said with a wry laugh. "We haven't yet decided what to do with you, but we will."

Misty magic soared past me. It hit the floor in front of the entrance to the passage and sunk down like acid, eating away at the soil and creating a big cavern I couldn't leap across.

Koko popped into view beside me. He crept past me, heading toward the squabbling witches, and a tiny snarl ripped up his throat. They'd eviscerate him in seconds. My poor little resha wouldn't stand a chance.

I reached for him, but he slipped from my fingers, scooting toward them.

Fear shot through me. I had to help him.

I might not possess much power, but there was one thing I could do.

This time, when I bound the scraped-away energy inside me into a tight, fuming ball, I didn't need to close my eyes. I wasn't sure I could do much with claws since it appeared I wasn't able to kill Maverna, but that didn't mean I couldn't land a few blows before the two of them cut me down.

"Ah, look," Camile said. "A resha. The king possesses them all, the stingy fae jerk." She stooped down. "Come to me, little one. I'd like to harness your magic."

What magic? Then I remembered what happened in the castle, how he seemed to know things, how he led me to the king.

There was more to Koko than an average pet.

"Grab him," Maverna cried, rushing toward Koko, who stood his ground, his fur bristling. "They're rare. Unique. And incredibly powerful."

I strode toward them, my hands lifting. Claws sprang through my fingers with a sharp snap, and Maverna stalled, her sister clinging to her arm.

Camile gaped at my hands. "What is she?"

"I believe we need to find out, sister," Maverna said. She swept her arm in a circle, and bars appeared around me, banging down to lock to the ground, encasing me like a bird in a cage.

Koko spun and raced toward me. He leaped, and when his paws hit the bars, they disintegrated in a puff of smoke. He landed against my chest and clung, whimpering.

I wrapped him in my arms to protect him.

The world shimmered, and we left the cave.

Chapter 10
Elion

Somewhere between Erleene pulling me from the cave and wherever I found myself now, I must've passed out. I woke on a small bed with a scratchy blanket pulled up to my chin.

I peered around the room that was only twice the size of the narrow bed, taking in smooth wooden walls and a worn braided rug on the floor beside the bed.

My head throbbed, and my guts ached, but strangely enough, the place on my leg that had burned since Maverna cursed me no longer stung. I carefully reached beneath the blanket, surprised to find the festering wound gone when I touched that area.

I rolled onto my side and sat, dropping my feet onto the floor with a thud. I wore loose trousers made of a soft material and a shirt much like what Raven might call a tee. Tucking up the pants, I peered at my leg, finding only smooth skin. The wound was finally gone. Had Erleene healed it?

Equally smooth skin met my gaze when I lifted my shirt. Erleene was known throughout the kingdom for her power. Only she could've healed the blow Camile dealt me. I'd felt her poison sinking through my belly, seeking my bones. If it had taken full hold, I doubted even Erleene could've reversed the spell.

My face, however, remained scarred, but I didn't care in the slightest about that. Raven loved who I was inside, not my outside, and that was all that mattered.

It was too bad she couldn't end my curse, but no one believed Erleene was Maverna's equal with magic. She could mitigate one of the witch's spells, but she couldn't do much to end it.

"Raven?" I called out, though I was the only person inside the tiny room. She must be outside, visiting with the others. I vaguely remembered Erleene agreeing to remove me and my friends from the cave once Raven freed them from the wall.

She'd released the king, Follen, and our friends, Bettina and Nuvian. And then . . .

I couldn't remember what happened after that.

Rising, I braced myself against the wall. My head spun, and it was all I could do to remain on my feet.

The walls sloped down on both sides of the room, giving the interior the shape of an A. Even the door had been cut to match, a narrow thing that would barely allow one person to pass through when open. I'd have to duck, or I'd nail my forehead.

Where were we?

"Raven?" I called out again.

I staggered to the door and gripped the antique metal handle, twisting it to release the latch and pull it open, but the door didn't give.

Someone had locked me inside.

"Hey," I said, the bang of my fist making the wooden door rattle. "Let me out. Raven?"

A memory slunk through my mind. Erleene magicking us from the cave one by one until only I and Raven remained. Then Erleene sweeping me away and . . .

Raven's hand slipping from mine.

"Raven," I bellowed, slamming my palm on the door again. "Someone let me out!"

By the gods, my mate. My love. My wife. Where was she?

"Raven!"

I kicked the door, each blow making the panel creak in the frame. I had to get out of here and find Raven. Erleene wouldn't leave her with Maverna, would she?

No. We needed her.

I needed her, even if no one else did.

My yank on the handle made it rip away from the frame. The door came with it, driving me backward. I hit the wall and rebounded off it, racing through the narrow opening. Outside the room, I peered to the left and right, noting doors on either side of an equally narrow hall.

The door to my right opened, and King Khaidill stepped out. "Ah, there you are, Elion."

How could he sound cheerful when Raven was missing, and someone had locked me inside a room?

I stomped toward him, grabbing his shoulders, something I never would've done back at the castle. But my wife was missing, and there wasn't anything I wouldn't do—anything I wouldn't sacrifice—to find her.

"Where's Raven?" I shouted.

"Ah, well, she's not here." His solemn gaze slid away from mine. "Did you know you've been unconscious for days?"

Unable to believe that, I shook my head. "It hasn't been that long. Where is my wife? Why hasn't Erleene gone back for her?"

"Wife, eh?" the king said, gently prying my fingers away from his arms with a wince. "Gentle, son. Gentle. I'm an old man. There's no need to be rough. You did say wife, correct?"

"We spoke our vows at my estate, but I can explain all that later. Where's Raven?"

"I think Erleene should explain," he said.

"You're right." Fury slammed through me, and I clenched fists at my sides. "Is she safe? We need to find her." I couldn't imagine going on without her.

"In due time," the king said. "And we believe she is safe."

"Believe isn't good enough." I started to storm past him, but he grabbed my arm. "That's not the way out of here, son." He tilted his head in the opposite direction. "We're inside an enormous tree. Can you believe it? And we're actually about a hundred feet—the human measurement, that is, and not one hundred . . . feet—above the ground. The top of the dwelling is open and last night, I sat on the decking there and stared at the stars." He sighed. "It was amazing. I have never seen anything like it. My castle—"

"I don't have time for this. I need to find Raven." I wrenched away from him and started toward a door at the other end of the hall.

"Well, I suppose we can have our much-needed conversation out there as well as in here." He trotted behind me and tugged open the door at the end. "Through here, please. There's a parlor at the end of this hall on the right. It was built in the center of the tree. Six hallways span the outer walls of the tree, with rooms in the middle. It's simply amazing, don't you think?"

Any other time, curiosity would've made me pepper him with questions, but not now. I had one purpose, and passing niceties was not part of my plan.

"Erleene is seeking Raven," the king said as he opened the final door on the right. He waved for me to enter a big, cozy room with chairs, sofas, tables, and even a tall fireplace within the center.

They burned wood inside a tree?

"I don't see Erleene here." In fact, there was no one inside the room.

"I just told you. She's gone after Raven." He followed me into the parlor and shut the door, thankfully not locking it.

"I'll seek her, and we'll find my wife."

"You were supposed to ask my permission before marrying any of the human brides." The lofty tone had returned to the king's voice, though his eyes surprisingly sparkled. "But I'll excuse you in this instance. It is clear to me you love each other, and who am I to stand in the way of something like that?" His shoulders curled forward in sorrow. "If only my own love still lived. What a life we would've had together, raising our son."

Frankly, I couldn't see how anyone would take joy in raising Aillun, but perhaps the king saw something different in his son, a side Aillun hadn't revealed to the rest of the kingdom.

"Sit," the king said, the tone of his voice stating there would be no arguing in this. He dropped onto a sofa and waved to the chair opposite a small table.

Since I had no idea how to escape this place without help, and he said Erleene had gone after Raven, I perched on the edge of the cushion and gnashed my teeth. There wasn't anything I hated more than lounging around when she could be in danger. I wanted to slam down walls and cross the inner realm if that's what it took to find her.

"We have something to talk about before Erleene returns with your wife," the king said. His lips curled up briefly before smoothing. "Wife," he said softly. "That means there's a chance you will one day have children, assuming the humans are as fertile as everyone believes."

"She's only half-human."

"What?"

"It's a long story."

"Which I would be delighted to hear," he said.

"This is stupid," I said, clenching the arms of the

chair. "The last thing I want to do is chat about Raven. I need her safe and beside me, don't you see?"

"I well understand." He leaned back against the cushions and released a heartfelt sigh. "I miss my own mate very much. She was everything to me. When she died, I wasn't sure I'd be able to go on without her. I wouldn't if I hadn't had my son. *Our* son. I don't believe you can imagine what it must've been like for me back then."

I wouldn't tell a grieving man his son was worthless. Surely he knew that already? Even his love couldn't be this blind.

The king rose from the sofa and strode around the table. He cupped my cheeks and tilted my face one way, then another.

"So, it is you." Tear filled his eyes.

Shock made my spine twitch. "What are you talking about?"

"You're my son, Elion," he said gently. "My true son."

Chapter 11
Raven

The cave disappeared, and I found myself in the inner realm. Clouds puffed around me, and as if called by the subtle sound of my arrival, a shriek rang out from closer than I liked. Creatures hunted here, and they'd soon come after me.

I picked Koko up from the ground and held him close. He'd brought me here; there was no way I could do this by myself.

Yet.

A world of possibilities had opened before me, as if I'd tugged open a door I'd never seen before and stepped into a magical realm.

The fae kingdom.

And I was part-elf.

I still couldn't get over the idea. How had my mother met my father and why had he left us? He was dead, and sadness made my knees feel weak. I wished I'd had the chance to meet him.

"How do we get out of here?" I whispered to Koko, not eager to call the beasts to me by speaking in a normal tone of voice.

He cheeped, and I winced at how loud it sounded.

When he struggled, I put him down. He scooted forward, somehow not falling through what couldn't be solid ground. Turning, he cheeped again. I knew that tune—he wanted me to follow him.

I took off after him as he rushed ahead, leaping from one cloud patch to another. Because I wasn't sure there was anything solid between the clumps, I did the same, gaining on him, though never pulling up beside him.

I spied a rocky outcropping thorough the mist, something that shouldn't be possible within the clouds. Assuming clouds made up this world. For all I knew, I raced through an alternate reality, or a world long forgotten. That's what it felt like.

Behind us, thuds rang out, and I wasn't confident enough about my dubious magical skills to turn and confront whatever followed. Last time I was here, I'd sent a beast away just by telling it to go, but I doubted that "trick" would work twice.

Whatever was behind us had picked up our scent or heard us, and it wouldn't stop until it had caught and consumed us. Somehow, I knew this as well as the back of my hand—when it wasn't sprouting claws that is.

Other dull thumps joined in, rushing toward us from the left and right, and it was only a matter of time before something caught up. We couldn't run forever.

If only I could find a weapon, though everything here

operated with magic, and I assumed I'd need a spell to stop whatever hunted us.

Koko kept running, shooting wide-eyed looks behind us. He raced to the big pile of rocks and waited for me to catch up.

"Can we hide behind them?" I asked, panting. I'd started around the side when he cheeped.

He placed his front paws on the big rock in front of him and looked up.

"Climb?"

I swore he nodded, and that was good enough for me. He'd brought me here, though I supposed this was the only place he could drop me after escaping Maverna and Camile. Maybe he knew how we could escape this realm.

I returned to him and lifted him onto the rock. He scampered up onto a smaller one, climbing, and I followed, creeping higher and higher up a rocky cliff that shouldn't be this tall as it hadn't looked more than ten feet or so off the ground when I approached.

But this was the fae world. Anything was possible, and everything changed in one blink.

Snarls rang out below us, and I peered down, shuddering when I saw beasts like nothing I'd ever imagined looking up at us. Some stood on hooves, while others had big, solitary claws at the ends of their knobby legs. They rocked on them, slicing into the ground.

Others clambered up the rocks like monkeys—the scary kind.

"Keep going," I hissed to Koko, though he was already six or so feet above me, watching me with dismay. "I'm coming." Where was he taking me? If he could pop us into this world, why not pop us back out?

He must have a reason.

He kept climbing, and I followed, scrambling over some boulders while racing around others, following spits of a path that wound up the side of the cliff.

Pausing, he waited for me to catch up. When I did, I looked down. Horror shot through me. The creatures had nearly caught us, the lead beasts maybe fifteen feet behind.

I scooped up Koko and bolted, racing around a boulder, hoping to find a place to hide on the other side.

Clouds obscured much of the path, so I missed the black hole in the ground, only seeing it when my feet landed where there should be rock but only meeting air.

We fell, my cry echoing around us.

I hit hard on my butt and slid down, falling into a black pit in the ground. I kept sliding, clawing at the walls with my nails and then my beastly appendages, when they magically appeared. Nothing slowed our fall.

Koko whimpered and nestled against my neck, trembling.

My heart ached from slamming against my rib cage, and my breathing raged in my chest.

Visibility was next to nothing, but I did spy a light below growing bigger.

We shot out of the chute and went airborne, soaring across a small cavern. I landed on my butt on the rocky ground and skidded to a stop.

Koko leaped from my arms and turned to face the

direction we'd come from. Would the other beasts follow? I had to assume they would.

I spied an exit from the cave and jumped to my feet, sweeping up Koko as I raced toward the opening in the stone wall.

Darkness met me once again inside a long tunnel with more light ahead. I tiptoed forward, taking care of where I put my feet in case more holes waited, my steps nearly silent on a dirt floor.

I exited the tunnel inside a large cave with a low ceiling and stalagmites sprouting up through the rocky floor. Turning back, I peered into the darkness. If something followed, I couldn't hear or see it yet. Remaining here to find out was not an option.

I hurried across the wide cavern, easing around the stalagmites, aiming for yet another opening on the opposite side.

As much as I didn't enjoy relying on others to save me, Erleene could arrive now and sweep me to some place safe.

How was Elion? The last time I saw him, he appeared mortally wounded. I needed to get to him and help him if I could.

I'd rounded a stalagmite two times my width and height, when something loomed in front of me.

I'd only seen creatures like this in books.

Was it a griffin? Or was the word spelled *gryphon*? Now wasn't the time to figure out what to call the winged lion with enormous claws jutting from its paws.

About the size of a horse, it had golden fur and an

amber ruff encircling its neck. Its furry tail ended in a golden puff, and its big, clawed paws would kill me with one swipe.

It must've heard me because it turned and snarled.

Its roar echoed in the cavern as it raced toward me.

I dropped Koko behind me and turned to face the beast with my heart on fire and my puny claws sprouting from my hands. Such a silly defense against an enormous creature.

Would shouting "go" work this time?

I shouted, but the beast kept rushing toward me.

Holding up my clawed hands, I whispered. "Please let it be over with fast. And please don't let it hurt Koko."

The griffin leaped, its wings spreading wide and its claws aiming for my throat.

Chapter 12
Elion

"What are you talking about? I'm not your son." I raked my fingers across the top of my head. "I don't have time for games." Standing, I bolted toward the door. "Tell me how to get out of here. I need to find Raven."

"Trust in Erleene."

"Forgive me if I don't."

"And denying your true parentage will not make it go away."

I turned back at the door. "You have a son, the less-than-wonderful Aillun."

"I will say that while I've done the best with that child, and I love him deeply. I am somewhat grateful to discover he is not my son and heir, however, because he would destroy the kingdom. You are my true son."

"I'm not your heir." This couldn't be happening. "I have parents. They raised me and my sister. They died . . "

The ghost of a memory teased through my mind, but before I could grab onto it, it was gone. I shook my head; that didn't matter.

"They died," I repeated. "And I inherited the estate. My sister inherited a smaller estate. Hers may not be as vast, but it is closer to the center of the kingdom, something she would prefer." Also, hers was not encased with ice. No, that was my curse. "Hold on. How does this relate to my curse?"

He gestured to the seat. "Settle down, son, and we can discuss this. I'll share what I know, and we can try to find a way out of your curse."

Funny how he hadn't offered that when he was unaware that I was his son. A sour taint filled my mouth, but I swallowed it away. He might not have offered, but I hadn't asked the king to help, either. "Would you have helped me if I asked?"

"I would've tried."

"So, that's all you'll do now. Try." I dropped into the chair with a sigh and scrubbed my face with my palms. "Tell me what you know."

"As you are aware, when I left you and Raven after we escaped the castle, I went to Maverna to discover why she was so determined to kill me." He shrugged. "I well understand wishing for power but killing me would not grant it to her. It didn't make sense, and I had to know why."

"Unless she hoped to achieve it through . . ." Ah, yes. "Aillun is her son."

"Indeed, he is. And since I was never with Maverna,

ICE LORD'S FATE

he is not my child." He held up his hand when I went to speak. "I was faithful to my wife and honestly, I haven't wished to be with another since she died."

I understood. If Raven was stolen from me—if she passed on—how could I stomach the thought of taking pleasure with someone else?

"When I found her, Maverna shared more than she should've. I confronted her, and she must've assumed I'd never be able to share the information she gave me. She confessed she'd given birth to Aillun within hours of my wife. She switched the infants, placing you with the parents you grew up with. As for my wife, your mother . . ." His sorrow-filled gaze met mine. "Maverna killed her."

The dream I'd had while I was unconscious . . .

Leaning forward, I shared it with the king—my father? I still couldn't believe this was true.

"Why didn't she just kill me?" I asked. "That would've been the time to end things." Was my curse somehow wrapped up in this too?

"She couldn't outright murder you," he said. "Your mother cast a protection spell on you, and there is no one who can diffuse a spell placed at birth, because it is infused with the love of a mother."

Sadness cratered my belly, and a sense of loss filled me. I hadn't known the women who'd given birth to me. "My parents were kind to me. They loved me."

"Maverna cast a spell on them to make them believe you were theirs. I'm grateful they didn't mistreat you."

This meant my sister was not my true sibling. She'd hated me since I was cursed. Perhaps now she'd be happier. That was all I could wish for her. We'd never been close.

"This means I have nothing," I said. It shouldn't matter. "Not even the ice castle belongs to me." I'd hand it over to my sister, though I doubted she'd want it, cursed as it was.

"You are my son." The king stood and came around the table. He leaned forward and gave me an awkward hug. Easing back, he maintained his grip on my shoulders. "I'm sorry I didn't raise you, though in spirit, you were the child I loved from the day you were born. It sounds odd, but I love Aillun as well, despite the angry, conniving man he grew into."

"He's your heir. You can't take that away."

"If he was a good man, I wouldn't. I have room in my heart and my life for you both, but we know Aillun has one goal. He tried to kill me. His mother helped because this would solidify her control of the throne. I'm sure he knows I'm not his true father. This is why Maverna cursed you; she can't outright kill you. But Aillun can."

"He can try." Would my mother's protection extend to whatever Aillun tried to do?

"With his mother's help, Aillun will succeed. He will kill us both and hold on to the throne forever with her power behind him."

"What do you plan to do about this?"

"I will scorn him from my life."

He infused his words with magic, and I felt it snap out before returning to the room, leaving only the taint of brimstone behind.

The king nodded. "It is done. Once the kingdom realizes I am alive, the scorning will take full hold. They will know I no longer claim him."

I couldn't imagine how hard that must've been for him. He'd loved Aillun. He'd raised an infant into the man Aillun now was. It must burn that he wasn't able to mold the boy into a decent man.

"And now," the king said, "there is only one more thing left to do."

I looked up, taking in his grim face and the steel in his eyes. They shimmered with tears, telling me how hard this must be for him.

Did I look anything like him or my mother? I wished I knew. I must've seen holo-images of the dead queen, but I couldn't bring even one to my mind.

I floundered, adrift at sea with no shore in sight.

Nothing felt certain in my life other than Raven.

"What will you do?" I croaked out. I rubbed my throat where the pain wouldn't go away.

King Khaidill grunted. "I will kill Aillun and take back my throne."

Chapter 13
Raven

Something licked my hand, which was totally not what I'd expected when the griffin roared and raced toward me.

I opened my eyes to see the big beast standing in front of me, where it must've landed, when it soared my way. But when our gazes met, it scrambled around me and raced across the open cavern.

Creatures from the surface slunk in through the opening. When they spied me, they shrieked.

And when they spied the griffin flying toward them, they turned and bolted back in the direction they'd come from.

The griffin huffed.

I grabbed Koko and slunk over to the wall, wishing I could find a weapon.

Koko cheeped.

"Shhh," I hissed. He'd draw the beast to us.

Seeing another tunnel to my right, I inched toward it.

The griffin roared and galloped across the cavern, aiming for me again.

I fled, running toward the exit, but I tripped over a rock and slammed onto my knees, barely keeping a hold on Koko.

Heavy footpads approached, and I dropped to the ground and curled around Koko, protecting him.

"Hang in there, little guy," I whispered. I felt like crying but held it in. If the beast intended to eat me, so be it. If I could do nothing else, then I'd protect Koko until the last minute.

He squirmed, squeezing from my grip. I scrambled to grab onto him again, climbing to my hands and knees, but he rushed away from me, aiming for the griffin.

I rose on shaky feet and rushed after my little resha.

Koko leaped and landed on the griffin's back. The creature's wings spread wide, and he spun, trying to dislodge the tiny creature.

"Stop it. Leave him alone," I cried, storming right up to the griffin.

His face rushed down to meet mine, but instead of biting my head off, he licked my forehead.

Ugh? His tongue was scratchy and incredibly wet. Was he tenderizing me before he ate me?

Koko cheeped from the griffin's back, and it turned its head to—I swear—give the resha kit a chiding look. Koko rubbed his head against the griffin's ruff and purred.

"Are you going to kill me or not?" I asked the griffin.

Why would I do something like that?

"Wait," I said, pressing my fingers against my

temples. "Did you speak to me?"

How astute you are, little one.

"You're talking to me in my mind," I essentially shrieked. My arms cartwheeling, I reeled away from the big beast.

How else would I speak to you? Griffins do not have the mouth structure to speak like you.

"Okay, so this is really weird. I thought you were going to eat me, but you ran past me, and thanks, by the way, for chasing the other creatures away. But now I'm here, my resha is riding on your back, and you're talking to me in my mind. Forgive me if I'm freaking out a bit."

You chatter.

"You would too if a big beast stood in front of you, speaking to you in your mind." My head tilted. "You do realize I'm human."

Part-elf, from what I can surmise. Other blood too.

"Yeah." I swallowed back my fear. "So you're not going to kill me?"

I am not.

"Then could you show me how to get out of this place?"

The cavern?

"This realm, wherever it is," I said. My hands shook, and my heart was on fire, but for now, I was alive. With a wet forehead, but I'd deal with that later, maybe with a washcloth if I could find one.

This is the inner realm. How did you find your way here, little one?

"The witches, Camile and Maverna, were about to

kill me, and Koko brought me here."

Maverna, you say? His claws dug into the soil, and I was grateful he said he wouldn't kill me, because he sure looked ready to rip someone apart.

"Please tell me you and the witches aren't great friends," I said.

We are not great friends.

"Say it like you mean it."

The creature snorted, and I took it for a laugh. Better that than killing me with one swipe of its paws. *She is an enemy to us both, it appears.*

"Yup."

Since your resha kit brought you here, I assume you do not yet know how to travel through this realm on your own.

"I don't. That's on my to-do list."

He dropped to his belly, and Koko hopped off, scrambling over to stand beside me.

"I don't have any magic except this." I held up my hands but, per usual, nothing happened. "I've made claws appear on my fingertips at convenient times. This isn't one of them, I guess."

You do not need that paltry defense here. I will protect you.

"Why? I'm grateful. Don't mistake my questions for anything but that. But why aren't you killing me?"

I do not eat meat.

"That's reassuring." Not really. I couldn't believe I was talking with a griffin. "You're gorgeous, by the way."

It dipped its head forward. *Thank you. You may call*

me Latarre.

Latarre, huh?

"I suppose I should go now." I glanced down at Koko. "We have to find our way out of here. I need to reach my husband."

You are married? he barked in my mind. *Who is your husband?*

"Don't shout." I rubbed my temples.

I apologize.

"I'm married to Elion."

Ah, the ice lord.

"I don't suppose you know how to break the curse, seeing as you don't like Maverna anymore than I do?"

Curses are a difficult thing to handle.

So much for that idea. "Yeah."

For now, I can do nothing about his curse, but I can take you to him.

"Really?" I breathed. "That would be amazing."

Hop on my back, and we will fly to him.

I gulped, but fear should never stand in the way of action, and I was ready to find Elion and break his curse.

"What do you think, Koko?" I asked. "Shall we let the griffin—"

Remember, I am Latarre.

"I appreciate your help, Latarre."

One more thing before I take you to the ice lord. Latarre dropped his head down close to my chest. When he exhaled on me, a small blue stone encircled with silver wire hung on the chain with the charm Elion had given me.

"What is this?" When my fingers touched it, it warmed.

A gift.

"Thank you, but I'm afraid to take it. If you give me a gift, I'll owe you something in exchange." I didn't know this for sure, but this was a magical place, and it was a solid assumption based on all the fairytales I'd read when I was little.

You will not owe me anything. This stone will serve you well when you are in great need.

"What does that mean?" The blue stone swirled, and tiny lights sparkled across the surface like it was made up of a night sky full of stars.

You will know what it means when the time comes.

Cryptic, but this was the fae kingdom. I didn't expect anything else. "All right. Thank you."

He touched my forehead with the tip of his snout and added a lick—I swore for good measure. *Climb onto my back, and I will take you to the ice lord.*

I picked Koko up while Latarre dropped back down onto his haunches. Once Koko was settled, I climbed onto a rock. Latarre stepped close, and I scrambled onto his back.

Hold on.

I'd barely wrapped a hank of his mane around my hand when his wings spread out from his shoulders. A few flaps, and he soared over the cavern floor, aiming for the tunnel opposite of the one I'd arrived through. He swooped into the darkness with only the sound of his flapping wings echoing around us.

A flash of light, and we soared above the tops of trees taller than multi-story buildings. Moonlight slanted across the world, and the call of nightbirds rang out in the forest below.

When a small meadow appeared ahead, he spiraled down, aiming for it.

I held tight and reveled in the ride. The only thing that could top this was lying in Elion's arms.

Latarre touched down on the thick grass and paced forward to the edge of the meadow.

I can go no farther.

"Where are we?" I whispered.

Ahead, you will find the ice lord. Walk up to the largest tree and knock. They will let you in.

"Elion is inside a tree?" I slid off Latarre's back, taking Koko with me.

He is indeed. Hurry now, before anyone lurking about realizes you are here. Many wish to harm you, little one, and it would devastate me if anything happened to you.

I patted his side and was tempted to give him a hug, though I had no idea why. "Thank you again. I appreciate your help."

Remember. When you need me most, call out. Do not hesitate, or all will be lost.

"I will."

He lifted off the ground and flew toward the treetops. A flash, and he disappeared.

I turned and, with Koko in my arms, strode into the forest.

Chapter 14
Elion

"I'll help you kill Aillun," I said, not at all stunned by what the king intended.

King. Sigh. Was he truly my father?

"It will not be easy." The grief in his eyes hit me in the chest like the hoof of a baishar, knocking the wind from me.

"He has been my son. Always." His voice deepened with pain. "But he tried to murder me to obtain the throne. How can I reconcile that in my mind with the small boy who once appeared to adore me?"

"I'm sorry." I had no love for Aillun, and never had, but it was clear the king grieved.

"It must be done, and so I shall have to be the one to do it." He stared down at his clenched hands lying on his lap.

My insides churned. I wanted to storm from the tree and find my wife. Yet I also wanted to comfort this man who might've been my father if Maverna hadn't played with fire.

"She killed my mother," I said, feeling the loss for the first time. Where my father was fair, though harsh, the woman who'd raised me had been . . . distant. It was clear she cared for me and my sister, but she had her sewing and reading, and we were expected to entertain ourselves. I did my own thing, and my sister tagged along, complaining about being bored. My father sometimes played games of favorites, and she'd gone for my jugular, always determined to win the crown of his approval.

She could have it now, though it was hollow because he'd died.

However, I'd hand the icy estate over to her the first moment I saw her.

"Maverna murdered your mother in her childbed, and for that, I will end her life myself," the king said.

He had a lot of killing ahead of him.

"I'll take care of Maverna," I said. "I owe her that and more."

"I promise. Soon, we will find a way to end your curse."

"We need to be quick, because I only have so little time left." The days were passing quickly, and I was no closer now than months ago to discovering the way to break it.

"She accelerated it," the king said with a scowl. "I will speak with Erleene."

"What can she do?" She was capable of doing a lot,

but what was she willing to do? That was the better question.

He grumbled as if he'd heard my thoughts. "Maybe nothing, and maybe she can extend it again. I will ask her to suspend it in some way."

"I assume she would've done it already if it was possible."

"She didn't earlier, because you weren't my son."

"It shouldn't matter. She should help me regardless of whose blood swims in my veins."

"As I said, I will speak with her," he said.

"I appreciate it, but I will speak with her myself."

He grunted. "You're too stubborn."

"I like to call it independent."

"Like when you married Raven without my permission."

I lifted my brows. "I control my own life as much as I can." The gods knew much of it was beyond my command.

"I would've granted my permission. I like Raven. She'll make a good queen."

I hadn't thought of it that way. If I truly was the heir to the throne, she would stand by my side if I ever claimed the crown—which should not come soon. I liked King Khaidill and would gladly see him rule for many more years.

I thought of telling him about Raven's relationship to Erleene and Follen, but it wasn't my news to share.

If anything, he'd only approve of her more. He'd facilitated the bride program and the truce, and he would've gladly welcomed a human daughter-in-law if Aillun chose one of the women. But knowing Raven was one of us in some ways would only add to her appeal.

"Ah, there she is," the king said, finally looking up with hope gleaming in his eyes.

I still couldn't call him father. I'd had one already, and despite our rough relationship, he was the man who'd raised me.

"Who are you talking about?" I asked, looking around the room that still only contained him and me. "Is Erleene back?" I jerked to my feet. "I hope she has Raven with her."

The king also stood. "No, I meant Raven is here. My daughter-in-law. I'm not sure where Erleene is, though she should be returning soon. She'll sense Raven has arrived."

A frantic urgency filled me, and my heart roared. "Where *is* Raven?"

"She's downstairs. We should go greet her."

When I yanked on it, I couldn't get the damn door to open, and I grumbled until the king used magic to unlock it.

"Stop pinning me inside rooms," I growled.

"It was the only way to make you remain still long enough to speak with you, son," he said with a twitch of a smile.

"I'm still not convinced you're my father." But the notion was sinking into my bones and taking hold.

"You will believe it eventually." He placed his hand on my shoulder. "I realize I didn't raise you, and I'm grateful to the man who did. I've heard he was a harsh person, but he did good with you, Elion. I'm proud to call you my son."

What would it be like to have a father who truly loved me? I wasn't a small boy in need of something like that, but the child who'd strived much of his life for his father's approval chimed up inside me and suggested *he'd* welcome a kind parent who cared. I shoved the notion aside. I had one goal, and it was reaching my wife.

I slammed out into the hall, finding it empty. "Where is she?"

"Impatient, aren't you?" the king said with a laugh. "There was a time when I felt the same for your mother. I still would if she were alive." His smile dropped off quickly, replaced by a grim sadness. "I didn't have enough time with my Lensa. She was taken from me too soon."

"Where is Raven?" I wanted to hear more about my supposed mother, but I had to see my wife and make sure she was safe.

"This way," the king said, striding down the hall. At the end, he opened the door. Stairs descended into the darkness.

Far below, someone knocked, and the sweetest voice I've ever heard called out.

"Is anyone home? Damn, this is weird. I can't believe I'm knocking on a tree."

Raven.

"Elion? Are you in there?" she said.

"Raven," I bellowed, racing down the stairs.

Chapter 15
Raven

The hottest guy I've ever seen opened a door mounted in the side of the tree. I'd seen the seam but become skeptical about this being a house when no one arrived to answer my knock.

Elion was mine once again.

I leaped into his arms, covering his face with kisses, and he swung me around, holding me close.

"Mmm," I said as I slid down his body.

He brought me to a stop so our mouths could connect.

Koko cheeped nearby, but all I could focus on was Elion. My husband. The only guy I'd ever love.

"You're safe," he said when we finally came up for air.

"I'm always safe when I'm in your arms."

"Excuse me," someone said from behind Elion.

"What happened?" he asked.

"She somehow held me back when Erleene took you

away. But before Maverna and Camile could do much damage, Koko magicked us from the cave—"

"Camile?" the person behind Elion cried. "She escaped my guards, did she?"

His guards?

I peeked around Elion, finding the king standing in the open doorway.

"Camile is Maverna's sister," I said. "Did you know that?"

King Khaidill peered around the woods. "We should speak of this inside." He backed into the darkness.

Elion released me, though his hand took mine, keeping me close.

I scooped up Koko in my other hand, tucking him against my chest.

"I want to hear everything." Elion patted Koko's head before tugging me inside the base of the tree. The door shut behind us, and for a moment, I couldn't see anything.

Elion's warm hand remained locked in mine, giving me reassurance.

Leaning close, he kissed my cheek and whispered in my ear. "After we catch up on what happened, I'm disappearing with you for a lifetime."

My heart thrilled at the thought of being alone with him again.

Unfortunately, I had a feeling we wouldn't be granted much time to reconnect. We had a curse to end, and I assumed, based on King Khaidill's presence here, a kingdom to save.

We climbed a long flight of stairs and exited into a hall that appeared to have been carved from the inside of the tree. Wood surrounded us from the rough floor to the walls and ceiling, and the outer wall curved slightly inward as the tree above narrowed.

The king led us into a large parlor that took up the entire center of the tree.

Erleene waited there with Follen, and they rose when we stepped inside.

"Good," she said, crossing the room to give me a quick hug. "Welcome. I returned to the cave but found it empty. A scent in the air suggested you'd gone to the inner realm, but I didn't find you there, either. I'm grateful you're safe, and I want to hear what happened."

I stood still in her arms, unsure how to respond to her hug. But warmth flooded me. She was family. Follen was family.

Tears stung in the back of my eyes. I missed my mom and sister so much. I'd barely thought about my little sister. So much had happened. I hoped to see her soon, to share that I was married and tell her I loved her. She was safer there, but a part of me was missing when we weren't together.

Follen and Erleene would never replace mom and my sis, but they'd come close. Over time, I had a feeling I'd grow to love them as much as those I missed.

She patted my back. "I know all this is strange to you. I only discovered your true identify recently. Follen as well. We knew our brother had died, but we never dreamed he had a daughter."

My heart ached at the reminder that he was gone forever. But maybe an aunt and an uncle would help make up for my loss.

"How did you discover who I was?" I asked, stepping away from her.

Elion watched us with concern in his eyes, but he didn't interfere. That only made me love him more. He'd missed me as much as I did him, but he'd give me the chance to speak with my newly discovered relatives before claiming my attention for himself.

"You have your father's eyes," Follen said, joining me and Erleene. "And this." He lifted my hand and flipped it over, revealing the birthmark on the underside of my wrist. Turning his hand, he showed the same mark on his own flesh. "Only those in our family possess this. You are not my daughter or Erleene's. That only left my brother. When I saw it, I was stunned." His gaze searched mine. "Welcome to our family, niece. I am sorry we meet during such troubled times. I hope we have a chance to know each other better before things become more complicated."

And they would become complicated soon. Everything was still uncertain.

His warm smile made any resolve inside me melt. How could I hold myself back from those who could love me?

Would it be weird to hug him? I couldn't resist, though I did step forward slowly, giving him a chance to back away if he chose.

He stood as I wrapped my arms around him, but then his body softened, and he hugged me back.

"I feel him with us when you're near, Raven," he said softly. "I miss my younger brother. We were close until he left our world to travel to yours."

"Why did he come to the human world?" I asked, stepping back.

"He was sent to begin negotiations for a truce, but it didn't come to fruition. He disappeared not long after he arrived, and many suspected foul play."

Was that why he left Mom? She never spoke of him, so I didn't know the details. A big part of me felt missing, and while I'd never meet my dad, I might have a chance to know him through Erleene and Follen.

"Let us sit," the king finally said. He smiled at us in turn. "I know you wish to share memories, but sadly, we don't have much time."

We took chairs, me sitting close to Elion on a sofa.

"Where are Nuvian and Betts?" I asked.

"I sent them to Elion's estate to continue exploring ways to end Elion's curse," the king said. "Nuvian has an idea that might work."

"What can he do that I can't?" Elion asked.

"Maverna is busy with us, which means she may not be aware of others entering her estate in the mountains."

Elion grunted; his face tight. "You hope he'll find evidence I can use."

"Exactly," the king said. "If he discovers something, he'll get in touch." He looked around at all of us. "First, I need to tell you the news I recently shared with Elion. He is my true son and my heir."

Follen's eyes widened. He gaped from Elion to Erleene. "Is this true?"

She studied Elion's face for a long time before speaking. "He is. I cannot understand why I didn't see it myself."

At her words, Elion's posture loosened, suggesting he'd held doubts until her confirmation.

He was the king's son? I peered up at him, wondering what he was thinking, but his face remained impassive. Only his hand shook in mine.

The king told us what Maverna had done to his wife and child, and how Aillun was not his true son. It was clear he was troubled about the latter. What would it be like to raise a child as your own, only to discover he wasn't actually yours? Some fathers would say love conquered all, but Aillun had tried to kill the king.

And that was the real difference. It would be hard to love someone who could so easily murder you.

"We need to return to the castle," the king said.

Follen leaned forward. "Absolutely not. They'll kill us."

A conniving look filled the king's eyes. "Not if we cover our identities with a spell." His attention fell on me. "How would you like to be disguised as one of the newly arrived humans coming to the kingdom to be courted by a fae lord?"

Chapter 16
Elion

"Only if the lord courting her is me," I said, my spine tensing.

"Definitely," Raven said with a wry laugh, her hand warm on my thigh. "There's no one else I'd rather play courting games with."

"There may not be much time for that," the king said. "If this goes as I plan, everything will be settled within a few days."

"We'll all go to the castle, I presume?" I asked.

The king leaned forward. "I need each of you to play a role. Aillun will be expecting my return, but he may not anticipate the rest of you arriving with me."

"You are my liege lord," Follen said, bowing deeply. "I will give my life for you, sire."

"I will not let it come to that," the king said, reaching out to pat Follen's shoulder.

"Disguised, there are many things we can do to help," Erleene said. "If you'd like, I could play one of the human women as well." A snap of her fingers, and her features morphed into that of a younger human with long red hair and rosy cheeks. She beamed and grinned. "Howdy. How are y'all doin'? I'm here to meet a fae lord so just let me at 'em."

Raven winced but smiled at the same time. "We could be besties."

"I like this term, besties," Erleene said.

"I thought you could work with Follen among the staff," the king said. "They're basically invisible. No one pays them any mind. They are allowed to go almost anywhere, and they hear things because of that fact. I need you two to be my spies behind the scenes, reporting to me regularly. You'll hear if our plan is unveiled."

"Ah, all right." Erleene's lips thinned, and in a flash, the redhead disappeared, replaced with the female I'd known for much of my life. Her eyes lit up, and she rubbed her hands together. "I'm more than happy to spy for you."

"I'll keep an eye on my sister," Follen said, the practical one in any situation.

"You'll need disguises," the king said. "Aillun knows you serve Elion. He'll suspect something is about to occur otherwise." His gaze fell on Raven.

Follen said scanned us all. "When do we leave?"

"At dawn tomorrow morning," the king said. "It'll take our combined power to craft this spell and keep it from slipping."

"What's our goal once we're there?" Raven asked.

"Killing Aillun is my job, though it will be a challenge to reach him," the king said. "I want Maverna's role in my wife's murder revealed in a way everyone knows. She must also pay the price."

"I assume you plan to reveal you're alive and accuse Aillun?" I asked.

The king nodded. "That will be the easiest way to do this. My thought was to appear during the ball he'll hold for the new women who will arrive late tomorrow. The ball is scheduled for the evening after that. This is why *you* will be an asset." His gaze fell on Raven. "I need a distraction once the ball is underway, and who best to do this but a human woman?"

"I'll help all I can," she said. "I assume you want something big enough to draw all eyes my way."

"Exactly."

"When eyes are turned away," I said, "you'll stride into public view and accuse Aillun of attempted murder and stealing the throne."

"My guards are loyal. They will immediately arrest him," the king said. "He will be tried and convicted, and his punishment will be imposed once I've taken back the throne."

"What about Maverna?" Raven asked. "How will you ensure she's punished? She's slippery, and she'll pop from view with magic, assuming she's there to begin with."

"Oh, she will be there," King Khaidill said. "Internally crowing about how wonderful her plan has come out. However, she will be harder to trap." His grim expression swept through the room. "The most important thing is ensuring everyone knows Aillun is not my son, and that Elion is my true heir."

"I don't want the throne," I said. It was important I make this clear. Maverna and Aillun must be punished, but I would not step into his place. If nothing else, the fulfillment of my curse would prevent this from happening.

For one moment, I actually felt sad about *not* taking the throne after the king had lived a long time. I hadn't realized I'd started to accept my new role in his life even if I had not yet accepted that he was my father.

Flint filled the king's eyes. "Once I'm gone, you can do with the throne what you will, but I *will* declare you my true heir. It is your right by blood."

I wouldn't argue with him about this. He was correct. As our king, it was impertinent of me to suggest I'd toss aside the crown, but I'd never planned for anything like this, so I felt disconcerted. My only goal had been to end the curse and spend the rest of my days loving Raven.

"You haven't mentioned me in all this," I said. "I assume you have a role I need to play?"

The king nodded slowly. "I appreciate your offer, but I don't like to separate you from your wife."

Raven's hand tightened around mine, and I knew what she was saying with the gesture. We'd just met up again. It seemed whenever we had the chance to be together, something or someone would pull us apart, though this was clearly valid. With Aillun on the throne, we'd never be safe, especially with Maverna whispering my true parentage in his ear.

I might end this curse only to have Aillun kill me.

But I couldn't hold back if my people needed me—no — if the king needed me.

When Raven turned her sad gaze up to me, it was clear she knew what I was thinking, what I had to say to the king—my true father, even if I hesitated to claim him.

"I will go with you," I said. "We will confront Aillun together."

Chapter 17
Raven

Elion stood. "We can talk more in the morning." He tugged me up from the sofa and into his arms. "I thought my wife was lost to me forever, and she and I have a lot of catching up to do."

"Of course, I understand," Erleene said. "When you leave the parlor, take a right, and climb the stairs two levels. When you exit, you'll find a large room on the left. I believe that will be more comfortable for two than the tiny room you were in last night."

We left, climbing the stairs. Anticipation built inside me. If we were in the human realm, we'd be on some tropical beach or hiking for our honeymoon, not plotting to overthrow someone who was trying to steal a throne.

The room Erleene gave us for the night was huge, taking up the entire level of the treehouse other than the hall outside the door. Screen-covered openings along one wall looked out at the treetops, and a light breeze filled with the scent of flowers and dewy leaves swirled through the room.

A big bed took up one wall and cozy furniture had been placed throughout the rest of the living area.

"I was terrified I'd lost you," Elion said, and in that moment, I saw the same vulnerability that drew me to him when he stumbled on the castle stairs and fell at my feet. As if I could make or break him with one word.

"I love you." I'd never say anything but that to my love. I breathed for him alone. I'd die if he was taken from me.

And that was a big problem. We had just over a week left—if I was calculating correctly. I didn't know how much time had passed while I was in the inner realm.

Whatever we had left was not enough. I'd fight anyone, kill anyone, to save him, but how could I fight something like this?

"If I kill Maverna, will that end the curse?" I asked, fighting tears. I didn't want it to be over. It would never be time for something like that.

"Believe me, I've tried."

"I should've clawed her harder, ripped off her head, and burned it."

"I love that you're so protective of me." He gathered me close and cupped my cheeks with his warm palms. "I love you. I would rip off someone's head to save you, too, love."

"It's not fair, but we both know that. It should never have come to this. She should've left you alone. No one would've discovered who you were."

"I stumbled into a cave where she was casting a spell. I don't know what her intent was with the spell, but I believe I interfered in a way that prevented her from trying again. Angry, she cursed me."

"She needs you permanently out of the way."

"And she can't kill me herself, thanks to the spell my mother cast over me when I was a newborn."

"I wish I could've met your mother," I said. Having lost my own mom, I could understand the pain he must be feeling. I'd had my mom's love and guidance until I was an adult, while Elion didn't have even one memory.

"I wish you could've too. From what the king says, she was an amazing woman."

"Will you claim him as your father one day?"

He shrugged. "It feels so new and sudden. I had a father, though he was strict and rarely showed kindness. Many times, while growing up, I wished someone else was raising me. And all that time, he wasn't my real father, though he and I never knew that. I guess that means he *was* my father."

"You're conflicted about all this. It's normal."

"It takes more than blood to make a dad." His solemn gaze met mine. "I hope you understand why I offered to help him. I can do nothing less."

"I do." I hugged him, stealing his warmth, his love. He was an amazing guy. He'd help the king even if they weren't related. "We have tonight, right? Let's make the most of it."

He lifted me into his arms and strode to the bed,

laying me on the soft surface. He helped me remove my clothing, and I did the same with his.

Soon, our skin pressed together. Only now did I feel complete.

He kissed me, the touch of his lips searing through me. Being with Elion felt wonderful and right. We were one, and as long as he held me, and I kept him close, nothing and no one would tear us apart.

My eyes stung, but my tears were not only due to my fear of his possible loss, but because what we had was so pure.

"Raven," he breathed, kissing my chin and my nose. "I love you."

"Show me."

I traced the muscles on his back, savoring the strength in his arms, while he kissed down to my breasts.

His fingers smoothed along my belly and down between my legs.

I parted my thighs for him, welcoming him home. Only being fully with him would make me feel complete.

When he sucked my nipple into his mouth, flames licked through me, centering in my core.

He slid his fingers down my slit, and I could tell I was already wet for him.

"Elion," I said. "I want to touch you."

He moved around until his cock was near my face and his mouth between my legs.

While he stroked me down there, he sucked on my clit.

It was all I could do to focus on giving him the same pleasure he gave me.

I glided my fingers down his rigid cock, but that wasn't enough, so I leaned close to him, pulling him into my mouth, taking all of him I could.

I licked and sucked on him as well.

A fever raged inside me and guttural moans ripped up my throat. I moved my head faster. He was big, too big for me to take everything, but I did all I could to give him pleasure, to show him how much he meant to me.

He did the same.

But I wanted more. Needed more. I wanted him in me, over me, and all around me. I needed to soak in his groans and show him with my body and soul how much he meant to me.

I pulled away from his cock and my whimper slipped out.

"Take it, love," he said. "Come for me."

"Only when you're inside."

He grinned up at me. "Your wish is my command."

He tugged me to the edge of the bed and lifted my legs, placing my heels on his shoulders.

Then he centered his cock at my core and drove himself inside me.

Chapter 18
Elion

There were so many ways I wanted to love Raven. Only when she was complete, would I feel the same.

My heart drummed against my ribs as I moved within her, driving myself slowly and then faster, savoring each moan that erupted from her throat.

I found her clit with my fingers and rubbed the firm bud, making it harden, and swell as her groans grew thready.

I lifted her thighs while I deepened my thrusts.

Her face revealed everything: the wonder of this moment, the joy of being with me, and the pleasure she found from our bodies moving together. I reveled in watching her, knowing she was mine, and I was hers.

"Yes," she cried. "Elion. Love."

"You feel amazing," I said, barely able to hold myself together. I wanted to spill my seed inside her and feel her inner walls clench tight, to know that only I could do this for her. "Mine."

Her lips twitched upward, and she gripped my forearms tight. "And you're mine."

"There's nowhere else I want to be, Raven. Only with you. *Only* you."

It was all I could do to focus on the wonder of filling her. With each thrust, I released a groan. My body tensed as I moved in and out, savoring the feel of how wet she was for me.

I rubbed her clit, teasing and tweaking it, because I knew she liked that.

My pulse thrashed in my throat, and I panted from my exertion.

She moaned while I drove her closer, her body tightening, then releasing as she trembled, beginning to spiral.

I would be with her then and until my last breath, giving her all of me.

I moved faster as she thrust up to meet me. Sensing how near she was to coming, I stroked her nipple, rolling it between my fingers while heating up the movement on her clit.

"Elion . . . I'm . . ."

"I feel you. Come with me, love."

Thrusting within her, I picked up my pace, my body smacking against hers. The muscles on my forearms bulged, and my face tightened.

She gasped, and her body consumed mine, spasming around my cock. Milking me.

I couldn't hold back.

With a groan, I joined my love, shooting everything I had inside her.

Unable to get enough, I loved her through the night, sucking in her sighs of pleasure while taking everything she had to give.

We deserved so much more than one night, but I stored each memory in my heart, holding it close. Once we were parted, me with the king and her on her own with only Erleene and Follen as back-up, I might not see her again.

Funny to think I could die while helping the king before my curse brought me to its own torturous conclusion.

Finally, we slept, and I held her.

I was still holding her when someone tapped on our door.

"We leave in an hour," Follen said through the panel.

Raven roused and gave me a soft smile. "Morning."

"Morning." I kissed her. I wanted to be with her again, but there wasn't time.

She stretched like a cat in the sunlight, then sat up on the side of the bed. "I don't suppose there's time for a bath."

This I could do for her.

A flick of my finger, and a large tub appeared, filled with steaming water.

She leaned back on the bed and kissed me. "You spoil me."

"If only I could do so for many years to come." I hated bringing up the loss we'd soon face.

Pain filled her eyes. She sucked in a breath and released it, then rose from the bed, her face loosening. "Join me in the water."

I bounded from the bed and swept her off her feet before lowering her into the bath.

Then I joined her, helping her wash, bringing out her moans of pleasure once more.

Chapter 19
Raven

I sat with Elion and the others for breakfast, then we gathered in the parlor to talk.

"We'll travel as close to the castle as we dare," the king said.

He'd told me to call him Ivaran, but I was going to find that a challenge. He was the king of the entire fae kingdom. But it appeared he was also my father-in-law, and I wanted to please both him and Elion.

"And split after that," he added.

"How will we get there?" I asked. I sat with Elion on a sofa in the living room two floors below our bedroom. Koko had curled up on my lap. He slept, periodically purring.

"There are a few baishars that can be trusted," Elion said. "Once we are disguised, they will know who we are by our scent. But the ones I'm thinking of will not share where we are."

Ivaran nodded, his face pensive. "Very good. The

spell we'll cast will not be easy to craft, but it will hold for several days. This should give us the time we'll need, but we must complete our task before it releases."

"Which means we need to make sure I slip in with the other women," I said.

"That's where Elion will come in. He'll lure one of them away, and we'll quickly cast a spell to turn you into her duplicate."

Elion grunted. "Luring won't provide a challenge. Shall we do it in the garden tonight? They'll be tired after traveling and retire early. This way, she'll be alone."

At least the garden would be safe now that I'd killed the creature who'd murdered my friends.

"It looks like we have the beginning of a plan," I said. "Let me see if I've got this straight. We'll cast a spell to hide us so we can travel close to the castle. Once there, Elion and I will hide in the gardens until we're sure the women have gone to their rooms. He'll lure one of the women from the castle and she'll be taken someplace safe."

Erleene nodded. "Follen and I will be waiting to take her to her destination. She won't be harmed, and she won't remember what happened."

"I'll look exactly like her," I said. "All I need to do is get through the events tomorrow and attend the ball, where I'll provide a distraction, and you'll slip into the room and show everyone you're alive. Once the uproar dies down, you'll announce Aillun tried to kill you."

Everyone nodded.

Ivaran leaned forward in his chair and braced his

hand on Elion's arm. "It will be over within a few days, and once I have Maverna in my possession, I will force her to end your curse."

Could it be that simple? The king was very powerful. Perhaps he could do what Elion and I couldn't. Joy almost made me feel giddy. It allowed me to dream. We'd have a full life together. Nothing would stand in our way.

We still had a lot to do before that happened, but it was wonderful to have hope.

"Let's do the spell, then," Ivaran said, standing. "Outside, everyone. After, Elion will call the baishars. Then we'll ride to the castle."

"What about Koko?" I asked, snuggling the small resha. "He can't come with us. Aillun will recognize him. Unless you plan to disguise him too."

"That is not a bad idea," Erleene said, frowning at the tiny beastie. "However, I doubt any of the women will bring a pet with them."

"He helped me," I said. "He saved me from Maverna and Camile, and he guided me when I was lost in the inner realm, but I hate the idea of him going into danger with us."

He watched us as if he understood our conversation.

"You are right to be concerned," the king said, his voice hollow. "I worry about the other reshas. Aillun did not like them, nor they him, and now we know why."

He wouldn't harm them, would he? "Hopefully, they're okay. We could look for them."

"We will indeed," Follen said. "It will be simple

when I'm among the staff to ask about them. I swear to ensure they are safe, my liege lord."

"Let's cast the spell," the king said. "And then we can decide what must be done with Koko."

We took the stairs to the ground, emerging into the morning sunshine. Birds swooped through the trees overhead, and the soft whir of insects floated in the air. The fae realm was one of the prettiest places I'd ever seen—and the deadliest.

I expected the others to join hands, but other than forming a circle, this wasn't like anything I'd seen in movies. Even Koko took part, standing by my feet, one of his tiny paws resting on my ankle.

"I need all of you to channel your strongest power and funnel it into me," Ivaran said, his gaze scanning each of us in turn. I started to step backward, out of the circle, when he cleared his throat. "You as well, Raven."

"Claws are not going to be much good in this situation."

"You have other power," Erleene said in a chastising voice. It made me squirm, but really. She might believe there was more to me, but I wasn't convinced.

"I'm only part-elf," I said. "The rest of me is plain old human and ... something else."

"There has never been anything plain about you," Elion said, his gaze full of warmth and support. "You have a special power that you haven't tapped into yet. It shines in your eyes, on your face, and it only adds to your beauty."

He could say the sweetest things, but I had no idea what I was doing with magic.

"Remember in the cave," Erleene said, "when you pulled from deep inside you?"

"Yes."

"That is all you need to do. That is your core power, the gift you were given from your father. Trust me, it will be enough."

"You can have it all," I said, not sure how much good it would do me. I had no idea how to use it, and so far, it hadn't done much beyond giving me claws. Although, I had released Elion and the others from their traps in the cave with those claws. Remembering that made me feel better.

I lifted my chin and nodded to the king. "I'll find it and send it your way."

He smiled. "That is all I can ask."

Since I seemed better able to find my power with my eyes closed, I shut out the world around me and searched for the ball of fire I'd used last time to make my claws appear. It waited deep within me, a tiny spark. I imagined myself cupping it and blowing on it gently. Surprisingly, it flared, growing bigger.

When it got to a size where I felt it would be of some value, I imagined lifting it and tossing it toward the king.

He grunted, and my eyes opened fast. I worried I'd scorched him alive, but he just smiled.

"You are more powerful than you believe, daughter," he said.

Being his daughter-in-law was such a strange

concept. I'd never wished to be a royal, but it was always nice to have more family.

The others fed him power, and he closed his eyes for a long while as we waited in silence. The air crackled with energy, and my hair floated around my face, though there was no wind.

Lightning lit up the sky, and a boom resounded overhead.

Ivaran's eyes opened, and he shouted words in a language I didn't understand.

Erleene's face and body shifted. In a flash, a young elf woman stood with us, smiling.

"How do I look?" she asked, swirling her light blue skirts around her ankles.

"Cute," I said. "This is amazing."

She beamed, turning to Follen who had sprouted a few inches, gotten thinner, and had long, dark hair threaded through with blue.

His pointy nose curled. "I have a feeling I do not look cute or amazing."

I laughed, and it felt wonderful to do so. "You *are* cute. And amazing."

His face darkened, telling me I'd pleased him with my words.

The king now looked like one of the troll gardeners I'd seen working near the bushes.

And Elion . . .

Only his eyes were the same.

A tall lord dressed in the height of fae fashion took my hand and bowed toward me, his golden hair gliding across his shoulders to hang across his chest. Since he was as handsome as a storybook Prince Charming, my heart should flutter from this gorgeous lord's rapt attention, but I missed my dark ice lord already.

"You will be changed when the time is right," Ivaran told me. He turned to Elion. "If you'll call the baishars, son?"

Elion lifted his arm and whispered something.

Thuds rang out from the forest to my right, and three creatures unlike anything I'd seen before burst from the woods, racing toward us. The bronze fur gleamed, and their silver manes rippled along their necks. Solitary horns spiraled up from their foreheads.

My breath caught at their beauty.

They stopped in front of us, steam huffing from their nostrils.

Elion stroked the snout of the lead creature as it shifted its hooves on the soft ground. "Will you take us to a safe place close to the castle?" he asked, and the creature gazed at all of us, one at a time, before chuffing.

"As for you, my little friend," the king said, stooping down in front of Koko. "I wish we could take you with us, but it will not be safe. Would you mind waiting here for our return?"

Koko looked up at me sadly before cheeping at the king.

I lifted him and gave him a big hug while he licked my chin. When he squirmed, I put him down, and he scampered over to the door to the treehouse. It opened as

ICE LORD'S FATE

if he commanded, and after one last look in my direction, he went inside.

"Will he have food there?" I asked forlornly.

"The tree will care for him," Erleene said. "It welcomed us many generations ago, allowing us to craft a home inside its heart chamber. The trees in this part of the kingdom have a symbiotic relationship with us elves. They siphon off a bit of our power, and in exchange, they give us homes safe within their cores."

Such an amazing thing. I wished I had more time to explore this. "My father grew up here?"

"He did." Erleene studied the trees for a long moment before sighing. "Life is simpler here. I hope I can return soon to soak in the joy of living among the trees."

Perhaps I could visit someday and learn about that part of my heritage.

"Are we ready?" the king asked, and we nodded. He climbed up onto the back of a baishar, and Erleene and Follen claimed a second.

Elion took my hand, tugging me to the third beast.

"You're with me, mate," he said as he lifted me onto the fae unicorn's back. He jumped up behind me, and his arm went around my waist, holding me close. "Would you like to travel faster than you ever had in your life?" he whispered in my ear.

"Yes."

My breath caught as he released a low, mournful cry.

The creatures whirled and raced into the forest.

Chapter 20
Elion

The sun had sunk low on the horizon by the time the baishars brought us to within a half an hour's walk of the castle. This was as close as we dared to let them take us.

We slid off their backs.

After quick hugs and nothing spoken aloud—though our gazes remained solemn—all of them but Raven started down the path leading toward the castle.

I patted our mount's face, and he exhaled softly. We'd been friends for a very long time. "Thank you," I said. "Be free."

After gazing at me for a long moment, he huffed to the others, and they raced down a trail weaving through the forest.

I took Raven's hands and tugged her into my arms.

"You even smell different," she whispered against my chest. "But when I look into your eyes, I see *you*, and that's all that matters."

"It won't be for long. Once Erleene has chosen the best woman, she'll reach out to me. I'll call one of the women into the garden. You'll be there, hidden, but ready to step out and take her place. They'll spirit her to a safe location, and Erleene will quickly return to take you to your room. After the ball, it will be over."

I said all this to reassure her, but I was also stressed about what might happen. This could fall apart within seconds, and I wouldn't be near Raven to help her.

"Love you," she said softly, and I hated that she trembled. But she had every right to be scared.

"Love you too. I will give myself to protect you. Know this." My heart came through in my words. I would lay down my life for Raven.

"Elion." She hugged me, and I tipped her chin up, kissing her.

"You taste different," she said with a snort. "I like it, though. It's still you." Stepping back, she held out her hand. "Let's catch up to the others and get this done."

We hurried and soon were striding behind the other three. Before we emerged from the woods at the north end of the castle, though, we stopped.

"Thank you," the king said in a low voice, bracing first Follen and Erleene's forearms. "We will be together again soon. When this is over, know that anything you might wish for is yours. I will grant it to you with my whole heart in thanks."

"Be careful what you say, my lord," Erleene said, though she smiled. "I might take you up on your offer."

He pressed his fist to his chest. "Anything."

"We do this by choice, sir," Follen said quietly. "No one wishes to see Aillun rule the kingdom." He looked at me. "And your true heir must ascend the throne once you have passed after a long life."

I wasn't sure I wanted to rule. It wasn't about making decisions or guiding our people, but I'd always seen myself as a simple person who enjoyed hunting and growing crops. Or I had until ice took over my estate, freezing everything.

It was no longer my estate. Somehow, knowing I wasn't entitled to something I'd considered my own gutted me. Where did I belong? Who was I?

My hand sought Raven's, and she took it and kissed the back. She knew how tortured I felt, and just by her presence, she gave me strength.

"You do not need to decide this now, my son," the king said. Funny how he could almost read my mind, but only a few of the fae could foretell the future, and he wasn't one of them.

He strode over to stand in front of me, and while his voice came out as that of a troll, I could see our ruler—no, *my father*—in his eyes. They gazed at me with warmth, acceptance, and a bit of love.

Was I ready to accept everything he had to offer?

Though I didn't speak, his gaze remained bright, which did more to win me over than anything he could've said or done. Gifting me with a castle or lands would not make me any more eager to accept him into my life.

But the warmth of a father's love?

That just might do it.

Chapter 21
Raven

I stared at the castle, waiting just inside the edge of the woods while the sun gave up and was sucked down below the horizon. Behind me, where the light didn't reach even in full daylight, creatures called out. Nothing came near. They wouldn't dare.

It seemed so long ago that I found one of the women dead in the fountain and followed Elion into the woods. Something had chased me while I was here, but Elion turned into a wolf and protected me.

He waited with me in wolf form now, also to protect me. He'd told me nothing would come near his wolf. That he'd rip anything apart if it so much as threatened me.

"Where's Erleene?" I whispered for about the thousandth time. "I thought she'd be here by now."

He huffed, but he couldn't speak in this form.

Stooping down, I pressed my face into his ruff, taking in his woodsy, wild scent. In his magically disguised human form, he wasn't quite my love, but as a wolf? Yes. So much, yes.

A snap rang out near the castle, and a low rumble echoed in Elion's throat. His tail stopped wagging, and he lifted his nose, scenting the air.

Erleene hurried along the path with a blonde woman trotting beside her. The woman stared forward blankly, saying nothing.

Follen strode behind them, watching, but if Elion heard or saw something, he'd let us know.

They remained close to the castle, moving through the shadows. Wise. If we were seen . . .

I didn't want to think about that. This was only the early part of the plan, but it would work. By tomorrow night, this would be over. The king would sit on his throne again. Aillun would be dead or captured, and we would be closer to ending Elion's curse.

As Elion and I stepped out of the woods and onto the clipped grass, Erleene and Follen led the woman over to us.

"We must be quick," Erleene said. "One of the other women made plans to visit this human, Diana. They are not true friends yet but have banded together since they arrived. I took time to spy on them all. This one has been the quietest, saying almost nothing until dinner or while she sat with the other women in the blue parlor." She frowned. "Although she appeared fascinated by Aillun." Her grunt slipped out. "Males with considerable power have always appealed to impressionable young women.

Other than watching him, she didn't do much. She didn't say anything important."

"Sounds good," I said, sucking in a deep breath. "What's the other woman's name, the one who's going to visit her in her room soon?"

"Marci," Erleene said.

Follen remained back, away from us, watching the path and scanning the side of the castle, though without moonlight, we must be too far from the building to be seen through the windows.

Erleene gestured for him to come closer. "It's time."

We gathered in another circle and this time; we fed our power to Erleene. She hissed when she received it, telling me how powerful the king must be. I'd thought Erleene could surpass almost anyone with her skills, but he must be even stronger than her.

A blink of her eyes, and I wore the exact same gown as Diana. I lifted my hands, taking in my medium-toned skin. My now long, blonde hair hung around my shoulders, and my feet hurt from the tightness of my shoes.

"Diana" would make sure the next pair fit.

"All set?" Follen asked, holding the real Diana's arm. She continued to stare at the ground, saying nothing, and I was glad they'd cast a spell to keep her from seeing this. I could only imagine how scary it would be to see someone turn into your double before your eyes.

"Wait here while we take her to the Trillafell estate," Follen said. "The monks will watch over her and keep things quiet. I'll bring her back once this is over, and when I release her spell, she'll believe she slept the entire time."

"She'll be safe?" I asked, nervousness making me gnaw on my lower lip.

"I will make sure of this," Follen said grimly. "Anyone who dares try to harm her will encounter my protection spell. They won't make that mistake twice."

Good. I wouldn't cooperate if there was a chance an innocent could be harmed.

Elion shifted back into the blond man and nodded to Erleene and Follen. "If it's all right, I'll escort Raven inside. I can be back by the time the king arrives."

"This is a change in our plan," Erleene said. "We won't be gone long."

"Let me do this," he said firmly.

She lifted one eyebrow but said nothing else.

"Shall we, Diana?" Elion said in a courtly manner, holding out his arm to me. "Allow me to introduce myself, by the way. You may call me Trevor. Lord Trevor Gulesk."

"It's nice to meet you, Trevor," I said, linking my hand through his arm and smiling at the game he played. I wasn't sure how I'd be able to smile again until this was over, and I was back in his arms. No, I wouldn't be able to smile again until Elion's curse was broken.

We left Erleene and Follen to spirit the true Diana away to the monks and strolled along the path as if we'd taken a random walk together, enjoying the crisp evening air.

ICE LORD'S FATE

Opting to enter the castle through the front door, we climbed the steps.

Like the day I arrived, I sensed someone watching, and I swore the person lurked in the shadows to our right. Then, it was Aillun.

Who spied on us now?

Footsteps rang out, and I gulped when Aillun strode into view like a vision from my worst nightmare. A purple bird was perched on his shoulder, fluttering its wings that resembled oil slicks. Patterns chased across its feathers as if something horrifying lurked there.

This had to be Maverna.

My heart stalled before picking up its pace and sweat jerked down my spine. Would she see through our disguises?

"Out for a walk?" Aillun asked pleasantly.

The bird took flight, and he watched it fondly as it circled overhead before swooping toward the forest, thankfully in the opposite direction of Follen and Erleene.

When Maverna became a speck in the distance, Aillun's gaze fell on me, drifting down my body. He gave me a short bow, and I swore he touched me. But he couldn't have. His hands remained at his side. "I don't believe we've been formally introduced, though I noticed you immediately when you arrived. I am King Aillun, ruler of the fae kingdom."

"Diana," I stuttered out. Damn, I didn't know her last name. What if he pressed me?

Thankfully, he didn't.

I swallowed hard. As much as I wanted to ignore the hand he thrust out, I refused to do anything to risk my disguise. Still, I flinched when he took my hand and kissed it, gazing up at me with a look that made my skin crawl. This was not someone I wanted to be alone with, and not only because I knew how slick and conniving he could be.

It was clear he wanted Diana.

Elion coughed, and Aillun straightened, shooting a frown his way.

"I don't believe I know you either," he finally said.

Elion bowed. "Allow me to present myself. I am Lord Trevor Gulesk."

"Where do you hold estates?" Aillun said. "I haven't heard of any Gulesks."

"Our holdings are quite a distance from here. Far to the north, beyond the Verdant Mountains."

"I see," Aillun said. He flicked his hand toward Elion. "You may go now. I would like to . . . speak with the lovely Diana."

"Lord Gulesk has agreed to escort me to my rooms," I said, making my voice flutter as if I was overwhelmed and thrilled by Aillun's attention. "I'm terribly sorry. As much as I would love to sit and chat with you, I'm afraid I must've accidentally eaten shrimp with dinner. I'm allergic." I pressed my fingers over my mouth and gagged as if my belly was preparing itself to spew.

Aillun backed away quickly. "Of course. Tomorrow, then, when you are feeling better."

"I . . . cannot wait," I said, clutching Elion's forearm.

"If you'll be so kind, Lord Gulesk? I fear I must lay down."

"This way, my dear," he said, guiding me toward the front door. A guard opened the panel for us, and we hurried inside.

The weight of Aillun's gaze remained on my spine until the door closed behind us.

Chapter 22
Elion

I escorted Raven to her new room, which was actually the room she'd been in before.

But I couldn't linger. It was important that I join the king.

Because I couldn't even tell with my magic if anyone was watching, I didn't dare say or do anything that might give away our secret identities.

When she turned to face me, her back to the door, I held her shoulders and tried to tell her with my eyes how much I loved her, how worried I was that this wouldn't go as it should, and to hang in there. That we'd be together again soon.

She lifted a trembling smile and her eyes shimmered. "Thank you so much for escorting me to my room, Lord Gulesk. Will I see you tomorrow during the events or in the evening at the ball?"

I dipped forward in a bow. "I would not miss the opportunity to get to know you better for anything,

Diana. Will you dance with me at the ball tomorrow night?"

"I can't wait." She flashed me a real smile, and I was grateful to see the sparkle of humor return to her eyes. "Perhaps I should be the one asking you to dance. I may have competition for your heart from the other women."

"I do not believe you have anything to worry about. My heart is already taken."

Her low laugh rang out. "You do love to flirt, sir, don't you?"

Only with her, but she knew that. "I believe I will make the effort to get out of bed early for breakfast. Will you hold a seat beside you at the breakfast table?"

"Of course." She turned toward the door and opened the panel. "Goodnight, Lord Trevor."

"Goodnight." With daring in my heart, I leaned toward her, whispering. "Sleep well, my love."

A smiled fluttered across her lips, solely for me. She stepped inside and shut the door, giving me a wink as she did so.

A scraping sound to my left echoed in the empty hall, but when I looked that way, I didn't see any cause for the noise. I strode in that direction, checking each door as I passed, but finding none of them unlocked. Only the one at the end opened, leading to the stairwell, and I thrust the panel wide hard enough that it banged against the wall.

Stomps below told me someone hurried down the stairs. I took off after them, though this could be nothing of concern. One of the staff could be returning to the kitchen after delivering a meal to a guest. Or it could be another lord leaving after escorting one of the other women to her room.

I rounded one landing after another, but I never caught up to the person. All I saw as I peered over the rail was someone dressed in dark clothing moving below. They hugged the outside of the stairwell, either by chance or on purpose—I didn't like that I couldn't tell which.

Eventually, I exited out into the hallway leading to the kitchens and other service areas. Elves bustled about, rushing from one place to another, even though many of the castle guests had retired to their rooms.

I spied the disguised version of Follen carrying a covered tray and caught up to walk behind him.

"Can I help you, sir?" he asked, stopping in the hall. He lowered the tray to chest-height. If I didn't know this was him, I never would've guessed. Seeing how well the spell held up made my pulse ease to a more normal rhythm and my spine relax. We were going to pull this off.

"I was about to ask for a meal to be sent to my room," I said. "Although I haven't been assigned a room yet, so perhaps you could also help me with that?"

He looked down his hooked nose at me. "We do ask that guests use a magical call to request something from the kitchen, not visit themselves." His sigh rang out, and he lifted a finger to an elf passing us in the hall. "Could you take this tray to the blue room, please?"

She dipped her head briefly, her gaze flicking from

me to him. "Of course." Taking the tray, she bustled down the hall, her skirt swaying across her ankles.

"Perhaps you could allocate a room for me on the third level?" Close to Raven, I wanted to add, but didn't. Would he know where they'd placed Diana?

"I can help you with that, if you'll wait here for a moment." He hurried back down the hall and entered the last room on the right, returning not long afterward. "I've secured you quarters on the *second* level. I do apologize, but all the rooms on the third floor are taken. If you will follow me, I will escort you to your quarters."

He took me to the foyer, and we climbed the stairs, exiting on the correct level. Outside the door, he placed his hand on the panel. "If you will do the same, sir, I'll magic it to allow only you to enter."

I knew all this, but it was standard procedure for new guests in the castle.

While I still had to meet up with the king, it would be good to have quarters assigned to me here. Then, if I was "caught" wandering around the halls and someone stopped me, I could tell them I was lost and ask for directions to my room. A ready-made excuse.

"Thank you," I said, entering the room.

"I will ensure someone is assigned to you, sir," Follen said with a bow. "As for a tray, I will have one sent to your rooms immediately. Would you like anything in particular?"

"No, whatever you have on hand will do."

"Very well. And would you like someone to magic you a bath?" he asked, backing away.

"No, thank you. I can do that for myself." I could probably craft magical food as well, but now Follen knew where he could look for me if he needed me.

Follen dipped forward in a formal bow before backing away. He hurried down the hall, taking the back stairs to the kitchens.

I stepped out into the hall, closed the door to my new rooms, and returned to the foyer. The king would be wondering where I—

"Excuse me," someone said from the right parlor as I reached for the front doorknob.

Swallowing, I turned.

Aillun appeared in the open doorway. "I wish to speak with you, Lord Gulesk."

Chapter 23
Elion

"I'd be happy to speak with you, my king," I said, striving to sound gracious. In reality, I wanted to bind him in spells and summon the true king.

I sent him a neutral smile as he turned and strode back into the room, leaving me to follow.

"Sit," he said, pointing to a sofa opposite the raised chair he took for himself. His elevated position gave him a sense of superiority he not only needed but strove for in every interaction. He might call himself king, and he may be attempting to rule the kingdom in some way or another, but Aillun had always come across as bumbling and conceited to me.

How long had he known he wasn't the king's true son?

Scanning the parlor, I spied six guards placed strategically around the room. They watched me, though I must not come across as much of a threat, because their postures remained relaxed. If they thought I might harm "the king," they'd hover, and their seeking and protective spells would snap down between me and Aillun.

I settled comfortably on the cushion, secure in my disguise.

"What can you tell me about the human female, Diana?" Aillun asked.

Nothing, but that was not the correct answer.

"I don't know her well, having only met her since she arrived, but she's kind and generous." And incredibly sexy. Raven, that is, though I'd love her no matter who she was on the outside. My soul would know hers for many lifetimes, as was common with true mates.

He studied his nails. "I may be interested in her myself."

No way in all the fates would I allow him near her.

"Oh, really, sire?" I said instead. "I could swear someone told me you weren't interested in forming an alliance with any of the humans." He'd called the program 'the dilution' to my face, actually, stating he would never consider mixing his blood with such lowly beings.

"What gave you that idea?" Aillun asked.

I shrugged, frowning. "I'm not sure I recall the circumstances, sire. As you know, I'm new to the castle. Perhaps one of the other lords mentioned it?"

"It doesn't matter." He leaned forward, bracing his palms on his knees. "Stay away from Diana. I've claimed her."

She had no interest in being claimed by him, and it was all I could do not to shout out the words.

"Perhaps the young woman has some say in this?" That was all I dared say. We were close to enacting the plan. The last thing I needed was to mess things up.

"She will do as she is told." A slick smile rose on his face. "I rule all, including her. If she won't . . . cooperate, I'll find another way."

He'd use magic to lure her. Would Raven be able to resist? She still wore my charm that should block spells, but it wouldn't hold out to true pressure. As king, Aillun had full access to the magic that came with the throne. Or he would once he was crowned. Had that happened yet? I hadn't heard.

"Do we dare risk the treaty?" I leaned forward also, as if I was contemplating luring in a different woman than Diana. "What if someone found out?"

"Worry about yourself, Lord Gulesk," he said.

There was only so far that I dared push this, but I would not allow him to try even a single spell on Raven. How could I stop him, however? I needed to be with the king, not chatting with Aillun.

"It was merely a thought," I said.

"One you do not need to have." Aillun pressed his back against the chair cushions. "I'd think you have enough to worry about already."

Tension coiled up my spine, but I remained still, keeping my expression calm. "What do you mean?"

He lifted his hand, and his guards came closer. "One of you get me a snifter of brellar and a tray of assorted cheeses."

A guard bowed. "Very well, sire." He left the room.

I watched blandly. How long would Aillun drag this out? I felt like we played a game, but I didn't understand the rules. He'd spring a trap, and I'd have no way of avoiding it.

"As for the rest of you," Aillun said, shooting me a sly smile. "Why don't you take *Lord Elion* to his new quarters in the dungeon?"

Chapter 24
Raven

I barely slept, spending most of the night pacing my room. I'd expected Erleene to show up to fill me in on what was happening, or the woman who supposedly had plans with Diana. But no one came to my room.

The next morning, I hurried downstairs as early as I dared.

"Ah, Diana," Axilya, the fae woman who oversaw the women, said. She studied my day gown with a tight expression. "You are much too early for breakfast."

"I thought I'd take a brisk walk in the gardens before I ate," I said. "I'm nervous." My high-pitched giggle rang out. "So many lords to meet today. What if I forget their names?"

"I suggest you repeat them to yourself three times and, if you can, assign their names to a feature. A lord with an overly large nose, for example, might trigger his name in your mind. Or one who is particularly tall."

"That sounds like a great idea. Thank you." I turned

away from her to cross the foyer, but she grabbed my arm, holding me back.

"I don't think you should walk alone." Her gaze shot to the door.

"Why not?" As Raven, I could think of a variety of reasons, but Diana wouldn't know women had died here. Actually, she might. I didn't know what the human realm announced about the bodies that kept being returned to them. Accidents, most likely, which would make some hesitate to accept the fae offer. Others would assume it couldn't happen to them, or they'd believe it was a string of bad luck that had ended with the last death.

"Why don't I grab a shawl and walk with you?" she said pleasantly. "I appreciate the opportunity to stretch my legs. I could show you some of the prettier gardens. Many are in full bloom right now."

"All right." I pressed for a smile. I'd wanted to look for Elion, though strolling around the grounds might not yield any results.

Where was he? My assumption was that he and the king were coordinating the final plans for the ball tonight.

Excitement sparked inside me. By the end of the day, this would be over. The true king would sit on his throne once again, and Aillun's reign would be over.

Axilya returned with a pale pink shawl draped around her shoulders, looping over her forearms. "Shall we?" Her hand swept out, toward the front door.

We walked down the front steps and took a right at the path, slowly winding our way around the castle.

"I've heard quite a bit about the human realm," Axilya said. "Can you tell me more?"

Where was Diana from? I didn't want to talk about my home state of Maine if she lived in Miami.

"There are many different countries with differing languages all over the planet," I said.

"And you came from which one?" She studied my face, but I only found neutral friendliness in her expression.

"The United States."

"Ah, yes. I have heard about that country. Have you been to Disney?"

"I have. It's so much fun. There are so many rides. It's funny because there's a castle and people dressed up as royalty, so much like the fae kingdom, yet different." Speaking about Disney would keep us away from topics that might not fit Diana's life. I explained about some of the rides, which she found funny when compared to riding creatures, plus the shows.

"It sounds like a delightful place. Perhaps someday I'll be able to travel there myself."

"I hope you can."

"Look at the blossoms in this garden," she said, gesturing to a large spread of bright purple blooms on our right. "Oh, someone has trampled some." Strutting over to the bed, she tutted as she lifted the bent stems, righting them. "Truly, people need to be more—" Her gasp rang out, and I hurried over to join her. "Oh, my."

"More broken plants?" I asked, wishing I could come

up with an excuse to leave her in the gardens and look for Elion.

"No, it's . . ." She turned teary eyes my way. "I need you to go inside and remain in one of the front parlors until I can send someone to collect you."

A chill shot up my spine. "I don't—"

"Diana," she shouted. "Do as I say. Go inside. Now."

I pushed past her and peered among the plants, but reeled backward, my lungs on fire.

A woman lay in the garden staring forward blankly.

Red marks encircled her throat.

And from the milky cast to her eyes, she'd been dead since last night.

Chapter 25
Raven

"Go inside, Diana," Axilya hissed. "Now."

"That's . . ." Horror swamped me. How was this possible? I'd killed the creature murdering the other women, but . . .

She straightened and grabbed my shoulders, giving me a shake. "I know Marci was your friend, but I need you to go inside *now*. Find a guard and send them to me."

Friend? This was why the woman hadn't visited Diana last night. My belly twisted into a knot. Turning away, I dry heaved, my body shuddering. Tears sprung up in my eyes; I couldn't hold them back.

It had started again. How many would the mysterious killer claim before they were satisfied?

We needed to end this now.

"I'll find someone," I said, fleeing Axilya and the poor woman lying in the garden. I couldn't get the image of her out of my mind. Like the others, red marks encircled her neck. A mythical creature tried to kill me, and I'd eliminated it. Was there more than one hunting at the castle?

Whatever the creature was that tried to kill me, it was sent by Maverna. Was she involved in this, and why?

I rushed through the front door and found two guards standing inside the foyer. I explained, and one ran outside to find Axilya while the other braced my shoulders.

"Go directly to your room and remain there, please," she said. "I will notify the king."

I didn't want to go to my room. I needed to find the *real* king and Elion.

I waited until the guard had hurried from the foyer before scooting down the hallway toward the kitchens. Bursting into the first kitchen, I peered around, hoping to find Follen or Erleene, but they weren't there. I spied Maecia, the elf woman who'd assisted me while I stayed in the castle. She was preparing a tray for one of the guests.

She wouldn't recognize me, but I didn't feel comfortable approaching her.

"Can I help you?" an older elf lady asked from nearby. Flour coated her apron and face, and tendrils escaped her gray hair streaked with purple that was swept up into a big bun on the top of her head.

"I was looking for . . ." Damn, I didn't know the names Follen and Erleene were using here. "Could I have a tray brought to my room and a bath?" Maybe I could quiz whoever came to my room.

"Of course," the woman said, her brow furrowing.

"Please, next time, wait in your room for a servant to help you. A few have been assigned to each of you and will check regularly."

"I will help her," Maecia said, approaching with a tray. "This is for you, Lady Diana. I was just coming upstairs to deliver it."

"Thank you," I said as the older elf woman returned to pound the mounds of bread standing in a long row on one counter.

A cacophony rang out in the hall, people rushing around and speaking loudly, telling me word had gotten out about the body.

An elf man hurried into the room. He looked around before rushing over to my side. "The king wants all the human women to join him in the green room. Do you need help finding it?"

"I don't, thank you." I nodded to Maecia. "I'll catch up with you later?"

She dipped in a small curtsey. "Of course, my lady."

I left the kitchen and strode to the green room, where I perched on the edge of a chair. Other human women sat in small groups nearby. They'd brought in many this time; I counted eight, including me as Diana. A legion of guards stood near the door, looking bored, and Aillun hadn't yet arrived.

On cue, Aillun strode into the room. If I expected him to look upset about what had just happened, he didn't. Maybe he kept stress like that hidden.

Or maybe he didn't care. During my first few days

here, he'd made it clear he'd be happy to sleep with us, but that he didn't respect us.

He took a seat on the ever-present elevated throne, leaning back against the red cushion lining the back.

"As some of you may have heard," his gaze locked onto me, "one of the human women has suffered an unfortunate accident."

"She had red marks around her neck," I said.

The other women gasped and stared at me with wide eyes.

"You are mistaken," Aillun said, his attention never leaving me.

A chill swept up my spine, and my flesh crawled.

I knew what I'd seen, but insisting he was wrong wouldn't gain me friends. It would draw attention, the last thing I needed right now.

"I apologize. I must be mistaken." I shook my head and drummed up some tears, not much of a challenge after what happened to Marci. I was also worried about Elion and the others. "I'm sorry. It's so upsetting. She . . ." I pinched my eyes shut, but that only brought her image to the forefront of my mind.

"This is a sad day for all of us," Aillun said. "But we must proceed with the plan. I'm sure," he leaned close to one of the guards and they spoke quietly, before he straightened, "I'm sure Marci wouldn't want this to interfere with your courtship of the lords."

I imagined Marci would.

Who killed her? I studied each face in the room, but they equally reflected shock and dismay.

Aillun looked bored, but that wasn't anything new.

Was he responsible? I wouldn't put it past him, though I wasn't sure what his motive could be. If he opposed the marriage plan, he was in a position to end it. All he'd have to do is say they needed a break after what happened to the women in the first group. Six months or more would go by before our governments asked when they could send others.

He had no reason to kill women. If anything, this made him look worse, because it endangered the truce.

"On that note," Aillun rose from his throne, "the ball planned for this evening will proceed as anticipated." His slick grin rose. "Ladies, do wear your best tonight. This will be your first chance to capture a fae lord husband."

Ick. When he put it that way, it sounded slimy.

The women tittered; Marci already forgotten. They might not have known her well, but she was a person like them. She'd lived.

And she'd been murdered. Nothing would convince me otherwise.

I needed to find my friends and fill them in on what happened, but I had no way of reaching them until the ball, when everything could go the way that we hoped or fall apart.

Axilya appeared in the doorway and clapped her hands. "Come, ladies. We have a busy day planned for today. First, we have arranged a light repast with a select group of lords."

Who could eat right now?

"After that," Axilya said, "I've arranged for a lovely

board game outside. Then, we must select gowns for the ball. If you'd like after that, you may retire to your rooms to rest in preparation for the festivities. So much excitement is planned for the evening! You will have a wonderful time." Her smile swept through the room as if she hadn't found Marci lying dead in the garden. "Follow me."

The other women rose and hurried after her.

I started after them, but the weight of someone's gaze fell upon me. Turning, I caught Aillun's stare.

I couldn't read his expression completely, but lust was among the options.

And anger.

Chapter 26
Elion

I paced the stone cell where they'd brought me the night before. After locking me inside, they left, ignoring my shouts.

Then I noticed Follen lying on a bunk in the cell opposite mine. Despite my calling out to him, he didn't stir.

Morning came, and Follen still lay on a bunk, silent. They'd done something to him, and I hadn't been able to wake him no matter how loud I shouted. Only his slow breathing told me he lived.

Something had happened to screw up our plan, and I couldn't figure out what it could be. Our spell should've hidden us from everyone, but it seemed Aillun had seen through it almost immediately.

I worried about Erleene and the king, and I was terrified something would happen to Raven.

Aillun knew, and he would track us down and pin us in the dungeon one by one. We'd never escape.

Again, I tried to open the cell door lock with magic. Like the other times I'd tried, my magic rebounded, hitting me like a bolt of lightning. I dropped onto my bunk to recover, rubbing my head.

Follen groaned, and I rose, rushing to the front of my small cell again. He stirred on the bunk, rolling to face me, and his eyes opened.

"What happened?" he asked, struggling to sit up on the side. "I was in the kitchen when someone came up behind me."

"Aillun must see through our disguises."

His body jerked. "Have you seen the others?"

"Not yet." Were they dead, or had they slipped the noose? My guts were on fire, and it was all I could do not to let the flames consume me.

Raven was at Aillun's mercy.

"We need to get out of here," he said, rising to his feet and staggering to his cell door. His eyes closed, and I sensed he also tried to pick the lock with magic. Like me, he reeled backward when the cell fought back.

"Are you all right?" I asked.

He shuddered but remained on his feet. "Yes. Let's combine magic and work on one cell at a time. Yours first."

I dug deeply, letting my power swirl through me, channeling it up and out to my door, though I waited until I felt his coil around mine.

We shot it at the lock. It recoiled and snapped back at us, and we both took a few steps backward.

But a click rang out.

My door creaked, opening the width of a hand.

I wasn't confident enough to touch it, fearing another spell would immobilize me. Returning to my bunk, I grabbed the dusty, holey blanket lying at the foot and wrapped it around my hand, using it to nudge the door wider.

"Yours next," I said as I hurried out into the narrow passage between the two rows of cells.

At his nod, I latched onto my power again, but before we could combine it, footsteps echoed from the stairwell to my right.

My heart leaped, and my mouth went dry.

"Back in your cell," Follen hissed. "Close the door, but make sure it doesn't lock."

Inside, I paced the length of my cell, ignoring the person coming near.

"Would you two like to get out of your cells?" Erleene asked with a grim smile. She no longer wore her magical disguise.

"Aillun saw through us," I said.

She nodded. "The first time he saw me. I sensed it and ran. Thankfully, he didn't catch me. I've been hiding in closets."

"Aillun played a game with me and waited until I was alone to confront me," I said. "He must know about Raven."

"As far as I know, she's all right," Erleene said. "He's sniffing around her, but he's left her alone. However, there's something else you two need to know. One of the recently arrived women has been murdered."

"What?" I yelped.

"She had strangulation marks on her neck that disappeared before many could see." Her sad gaze met mine. "Raven and Axilya found her in the garden."

"I suspected someone has been murdering them all along," Follen said. "We need to get Raven out of here and warn the other women."

"Who do you think is killing them?" I asked him.

His grim gaze met mine. "Maverna, naturally, but I believe Aillun could also be involved."

"They never wanted the truce," I said. "Murdering the women would end it for sure."

"Yet they're calling it an accident for some reason," Erleene said. "If they're responsible, we'll prove it and make them pay."

They had so much to pay for.

Erleene shook her head. "As for getting you out of here—" She peered over her shoulder before turning her panicked gaze back to us. A shudder ripped through her, and she gazed about wildly. "Someone's coming."

A pop, and she disappeared, I assumed, into the inner realm. Since locations were fluid when a person traveled there, she may not be able to return here immediately. She'd probably have to exit somewhere nearby and make her way back here on foot.

She'd be in considerable danger all the time.

The footsteps grew louder.

Follen dropped down onto his bunk and turned his back to the door, pretending to still be unconscious.

I sat on my bunk and waited to see who was coming,

biting back my snarl when Aillun strode into view with a small group of guards flanking him.

"So, Elion," Aillun said, sauntering close to my cell door. He grinned to see me trapped inside. But when his gaze shot to Follen, he huffed. "He was your servant, wasn't he?"

"His name is Follen," I said.

"I don't bother remembering the names of elves. They exist merely to serve the fae."

I'd never understood why he maintained such an elitist attitude. The fae had ruled for many generations only by the grace of the elves. Many were more powerful than us. They could take control away from us if they chose. So it had been for longer than most remembered, and so it would likely be for many generations to come.

"I didn't come here to speak of staff," he said. "I'm looking for someone in particular, and I believe you may know where he is."

"I'm not sure who you're talking about."

"Where is the king?" he barked.

I lifted my eyebrows. It was bold of him to let the guards know the king still lived. But their gazes remained locked on the wall, telling me Aillun had cast spells to make them cooperate no matter what they heard or saw.

"Didn't you accuse me of killing him?" I asked.

He glanced at Follen again. "Some fae have a way of slipping the noose."

"I don't know where the king is."

"Yet you come here, bumbling around in a simple disguise that even a low-level witch could see through."

It had been a complex spell. We'd just underestimated Aillun's powers.

"Did Maverna help you with that?" I asked.

The flash of irritation crossing his face gave me my answer.

"Where is he?" he snarled, his hands lifting.

I was lifted off the bunk and yanked forward. Smacking into the bars, I bit back a grunt of pain.

Aillun pressed himself against the other side of the bars, shoving his face in between them. When the door creaked open, rage filled his face. He yanked the door shut, and the lock clicked.

"Tell me where he is," he hissed. "If you do, I might be lenient with you."

"As lenient as when you planned to murder me in public for killing the king?"

He snarled and lifted me again, flinging me against the right wall.

I hit it hard and slumped down onto the stone floor.

The world spun, and I didn't know anything after that.

Chapter 27
Raven

At breakfast, I sat beside Lord Iolas. I'd first met him when he came to the diner where I worked. Elion and two other lords sat with him, and I'd served them breakfast. That was when I suspected Elion would be an important person in my life.

As Diana, I struggled to respond to Lord Iolas's attention like she would, when all I wanted was to be safe within Elion's arms. With so little time remaining until this was finished, I worried something would go wrong.

Aillun presided over us, eating little and watching us each in turn from his gilded chair at the end of the long table. I swore his gaze lingered on me the most, and it not only creeped me out, but it also frightened me.

This guy held all the power in the kingdom. If he crooked his finger my way, I wouldn't be allowed to refuse him. But I was less concerned about him trying to seduce me than him seeing through my disguise.

If he did, he'd accuse me, wouldn't he? Surely, he wouldn't toy with me like a cat with a cricket.

I hadn't expected to see Elion before I completed my side of the mission at the ball, but that didn't mean I wasn't anxious about something happening to him. So much relied on the king outing Aillun tonight, and almost anything could make this fall apart.

Fear stormed through my mind as I struggled to eat and chat with Iolas and Lord Ethar, seated on my other side at the table.

Finally, everyone finished eating. Aillun rose and left the room, not sparing me a glance, and my pulse settled to a steadier rhythm. I only needed to get through today and get to the ball, and this would be over.

Then Elion and I could find a way to break his curse. I was at a loss for how to do it, but there must be a way.

"Will you be my partner during the upcoming game?" Iolas asked eagerly, his blue eyes alight with interest.

"No, I believe she will be my partner," Ethar said in jest, though his flinty gaze speared Iolas.

"Perhaps I should play the game with both of you?" I said, grateful to see Axilya rising from where she sat on the opposite side of the table. She'd sweep us away, explain the game, and I could find a way through it. Each event was one less I had to participate in.

Iolas grumbled. Ethar grinned. But before he could speak again, Axilya cleared her throat.

"Ladies," she said, smiling benignly around the table. One of the women tittered, and a few others joined in. "If you would follow me to the everlorn parlor, I will explain what you can expect today. Lords? If you would be so kind as to meet up with us on the side lawn in fifteen minutes, we shall play a game and you can get to know the women better."

The lords grumbled good-naturedly while the women rose and followed Axilya from the room.

Inside the everlorn parlor, Axilya took a seat on a big sofa, waving to the other furniture in the room. "Sit. I wish to speak to you all before we rejoin the lords."

I settled beside a woman with gorgeous long red hair. She wore a green gown that made her peaches and cream complexion glow. Her soft smile took me in, and she took my hand and squeezed it. Like when I arrived in the fae kingdom as myself, many of us clung together, seeking a connection with home. Then things started going haywire.

"We mourn the loss of Marci," Axilya said.

The woman who'd died.

"But a tragic accident must not hold us back. The truce demands matches between human women and fae men, and that is why you are here." Axilya flashed us a sincere smile, and I was grateful she wasn't conniving like Camile. "The game you're about to play requires a partner, and while it will be tempting to choose from among yourselves, you're here to meet the lords. Select one, get to know him, and if he isn't a good fit, choose another. They are eager to meet you. All of us in the fae kingdom wish for you to be happy with whomever you wed, so take the time you need before announcing your pick.

Remember, while it may be possible to end your marriage in the future, our hope is that you will find lasting love."

And have babies. The fae birthrate had dropped off considerably, and it was hoped our blood could give the birthrate a boost. A stark proposition, but it was part of the agreement. Birth control was forbidden until matches had produced at least one child.

A few of the women sighed, tremulous smiles rising on their faces at the thought of being courted by fae lords and having babies.

The redhead shot me a grin before leaning close to whisper. "I'm Wren, by the way, and I've already chosen who I want to marry."

I frowned. "So soon?"

"When you know, you know. Zyan's hot, and I think he's just as interested in me as I am in him."

"I'm happy for you." I hoped a relationship developed within such a short timespan worked out. More power to her.

I'd essentially done the same thing with Elion.

"The game you are about to play is called Wellalee," Axilya said. "In the game, you will need to move your ball through the course, avoiding pitfalls and . . . unexpected events."

"Really?" A dark-haired woman said, pushing her back against the sofa cushion. "Like, is this some kind of Hunger Games, fae version?"

"Really, Danica," Axilya said. "I'm not completely sure what you mean by Hungry Games, but your tone gives me an idea. You will not be in danger during this game. It's fun, something to be enjoyed with the fae lord you choose as your partner. It might give you an opportunity to see how he responds to a win or a loss. However, I believe the best way to learn how to win a game is to play it. All the lords know this game, and they will be happy to share further details."

"You said you'd explain the rules," Danica said.

"And that was a lovely excuse to separate you from them, was it not? I brought you here to give the last of the lords a chance to arrive and meet us outside. We will proceed to that location where you will choose a partner and then we shall play. Any questions?"

We all shrugged and rose, following her through the halls to the right side of the building. We exited out onto a broad deck with stairs on either side that looked out over a broad stretch of clipped lawn.

A game unlike anything I'd seen before had been set up in front of us, taking up at least three acres. A bunch of fae guys milled around to the right of the game.

"Wow," Danica said, her eyes wide. "It looks like something out of ancient Egypt."

"An apt description," Axilya said. She clapped her hands. "Choose your partner, and we shall begin. Whichever of you wins today's event, by the way, will be presented with a small estate in the mountains of Vustine, one of the loveliest parts of the kingdom."

One of the women in my group had won that estate, but she'd left the kingdom. I guess that meant it was up for grabs again. Would someone remain here long enough to claim it this time?

"A *real* estate?" Wren asked.

"Yes," Axilya said with a dip of her head. "Perhaps it will be yours."

Wren's face flushed. "We'll see. Maybe I won't need an estate." Her gaze fell on one of the lords waiting below us on the lawn. I didn't recognize him from before. Maybe he was a new arrival.

"It is time, ladies," Axilya said, sweeping her hand out.

We left the deck and strolled among the lords. My heart pinched because I didn't want to pick one, even if it was only pretend. I wanted to be with Elion in a place where we could be safe, a place where we could love each other and grow old together.

"I believe you will play this game with me," someone said from behind me.

I didn't need to look, though I cringed.

Aillun's sweaty palm dropped onto my shoulder.

Chapter 28
Elion

In a dream, I crept through the hallways of my family estate.

"Where are you going?" my younger sister asked from behind me in a voice higher than I remembered.

I turned to find her standing on the opposite end of the hall dressed in a gown suited for the eleven-year-old she was.

A memory? If so, I'd forgotten it.

Or buried it.

"I do not wish for company," I said. "Leave me alone."

She skipped down the hall to join me, poking my chest when she reached me.

I'd also forgotten how she always took teasing in a mean direction.

"You will take me with you," she said. "We can play."

My lips twisted. "I do not wish to entertain you, Truella."

Her foot whipped forward, kicking me hard in the shin.

"Mother," she cried, her voice rising to a fever-pitch. "Mother! Elion is being mean. He refuses to play with me."

"Elion," our mother called out from the parlor on our right, her voice filled with exasperation. "Could you please be nice to your sister? She is bored. Entertain her."

"I do not wish to play with her," I said. Surely my needs mattered as much as hers.

"That does not matter," Mother said. "Find something to do together, would you?"

Grumbling, I poked her shoulder, though not as hard as she'd kicked me. My leg still ached, but I wasn't mean.

"I'm going for a walk around the estate," I said.

"Good." Her sly smile rose. "I shall go along with you."

I huffed and continued down the hall with her tagging along. At fifteen, I felt almost grown up. The last thing I wanted to do was entertain my sister.

"I am not going to talk with you," I said, crossing the foyer to the front door.

"Good. I do not need you to do so."

I stopped, my hand on the door. "Then why are you so determined to follow me?"

"I am bored," she said. "You have more fun than me."

It didn't seem that way to me. Mother and father doted on Truella, though I didn't feel slighted about it very often. They took her to places more than me, and I liked being by myself. If they traveled alone, they brought *her* gifts. Dolls—though I didn't want one of those. Toys from distant places. And once a baby eradone. She'd let that go free, and we never saw it again.

Whatever they gave me felt more like afterthoughts. A book about ships. Chocolates with one piece missing from the box. The best of them all was a scribbliera I wasn't sure what to do with. Only grownups used those.

We left through the front door and took the steps to the ground. I turned right and strode around the big building, kicking stones off the path while Truella picked flowers from the garden on our right, snatching one blossom after another before skipping to catch up with me. Eventually, she had a big bunch of them she kept stuffing into her face for sniffing.

"I love flowers, don't you, Elion?" she said.

I rolled my eyes. "Flowers are boring."

"Here." She pushed them into my face. "Smell them."

Shaking my head, I backed away and continued along the path. It left the building and continued up a long hill where I raced through the woods with my sister following. Eventually, I slowed my pace.

She snarled and smacked my arm with the flowers, which was better than sniffing them. "Slow down. I cannot keep up."

We walked through the woods for some time, coming to a field where I would often lie in the deep grass and dream of being a soldier. I'd once heard there was a small house somewhere in the woods beyond, but when I sought it, I'd never found it.

We reached the broad meadow and I sat down.

Truella slumped down beside me, stretching out her legs.

Grass taller than both of us wavered around us. She plucked strands one by one and began weaving them into a signet. If I knew her, she'd wear it to dinner and our parents would commend her on her craftsmanship before asking me what I had to show for my day.

"Nothing," I'd say. "I did nothing."

She hummed, swaying her feet back and forth.

I decided it wasn't *that* horrible spending time with my sister. She must be as bored as me. Nothing much happened at our estate to make one day feel any different from another.

Her incessant humming bothered me, however, but I held my patience. She was a child, and she was entertaining herself, which was better than demanding I do it for her.

Eventually, she tossed her weaving away. "I am bored."

"You wished to come with me." I lay back in the grass, staring at the clouds. "This is what I wanted to do. Do not complain now."

"Take me back." She rose to her feet, glaring down at me.

"Find your own way back."

A sneer twisted her lips. "I will tell Mother you left me in the woods, that I was frightened."

With a heavy sigh, I rose and walked with her until the castle loomed below us. "Go from here on your own."

"If I want to make you—"

I held up my hand. "Enough. I brought you back. Leave me alone."

She huffed. "Go lay in the field. You are boring." She pivoted and raced toward the castle.

Despite my wish to ignore her, I did want her safe. I waited until she'd entered through a back door, then returned to my field.

Finally, I could dream about being a soldier.

I must've dozed because something woke me.

Soft voices drifted from the forest along the side of the meadow.

A path left that part of the forest and continued through the open area, the grass in that section tamped down by the passage of many feet. Eventually, it exited out onto the back lawn of our estate. It also passed close to where I sat.

I might be able to see who it was without them seeing me. Otherwise, I could creep up behind them and spy on them like a good soldier would do. This would be the true adventure I'd longed for.

At least Truella was not here any longer, humming to give away my soldier location. With a stick in hand, my pretend sword, I waited, my heart thrumming with anticipation.

As the voices grew louder, I picked out my father's. I wasn't sure who he spoke with. A woman? It didn't sound like Mother, and besides, she must still be sitting in the front parlor.

The woman laughed, high-pitched and somewhat irritating.

My father didn't seem to think so, since his own laugh rang out, deep and almost seductive. I wasn't sure why I thought of it that way. It just was.

I'd never been with a female, though one of the staff had tried to slink into my bedroom one night about a year ago. I'd sent her away, more embarrassed than intrigued by the notion of inviting her to my bed.

Normally, I'd rise to my feet, tell my father I was here, and speak with him.

He told us he'd be away for a few days. Maybe he'd come home early and brought a guest.

Their footsteps grew louder as they approached on the path.

They stopped not far from where I sat, spying through the thick grass.

My father walked with a woman I'd only seen once before, though I didn't remember her name. At the time, she'd visited with an old man. Her husband? I couldn't remember. I hadn't cared then.

I cared now.

They stopped and faced each other not far from where I remained hidden.

She slid her fingers along my father's neck, tugging his head down to meet hers in a kiss.

With a moan, she wrapped her body around his.

Chapter 29
Raven

"Oh, um, King Aillun," I said, my pulse and voice fluttering. "I'm terribly sorry, but I already promised to play this game with Lord Iolas."

Poor Lord Iolas blanched and looked ready to bolt for the hills.

He blinked before breaking away from the other guys. "I'm sure King Aillun would rather—"

"No, please," I said, easing out from beneath Aillun's grip and joining Iolas. "I'm so looking forward to you explaining the rules."

Iolas yanked on the hem of his tunic, his worried gaze shooting to Aillun. "I don't think . . ." His face scrunched up, and he spun on his heel and raced for the castle.

"It appears your partner has other plans," Aillun said slickly, his hand stretching out to grab my arm.

"As does Diana," someone said. I turned to find a tall, slender lord with graying hair at his temples. He had teal-colored eyes I'd recognize anywhere.

Latarre. When I'd last seen him, he was in griffin form. Was he some kind of shifter? He must recognize me, or maybe this was just a wonderful coincidence, him being here at the right time.

"Do I know you?" Aillun asked, looking down his nose at Latarre. "You are not familiar to me."

Latarre bowed, keeping it short. I'd learned a bit about fae bows since I came here. A deep bow showed deference. A shallow one did not.

"I am Lord Latarre Neribellen Alosrin," he said with equal haughtiness. "Surely you must know of my family name if not me."

The subtle sneer did not leave Aillun's face. "I do not know any Alosrins."

"This is a true loss," Latarre said gravely. "Our estates are not large, however, and far from here, so I suppose I am not too surprised."

"I will ask about you," Aillun said. "Discover if you harbor any . . . secrets."

One of Latarre's graying eyebrows lifted. "Naturally, and no, I do not."

"Since I do not know you," Aillun's voice came out pinched, "you will not play this game with Diana."

"Do I have a say in this?" I asked politely.

One of the women standing nearby gasped, while the lords fluttering around the women gaped. With so few women choosing lords, they watched everything we did. They'd even judge Aillun if he didn't behave.

I could tell their stares pissed him off by his eyes darkening and the scowl denting his forehead.

He grunted and took a step backward. "You will dance with me at the ball tonight, Diana."

It was a demand, not a request.

Deciding grace needed to rule in this confrontation, I gave a soft smile and dipped into a deep curtsy. "Of course, my king. I would be delighted to do so. Shall I save you the first dance?"

Aillun straightened his tunic and slicked his hands across his hair. "That will do nicely." His gaze traveled down my front, lingering on my breasts.

My spine twitched.

Latarre released a low growl.

"Until later, then," Aillun said with a nod. His penetrating gaze studied Latarre before he moved around us and returned to the balcony. I hoped he'd slink inside in defeat, but he stood on the upper level instead, watching me.

I leaned close to Latarre and dropped my voice. "Thank you."

"You're very welcome," he said. "I got the impression you were not eager to play the game with Aillun."

I shuddered. "I'm not eager to do anything with him."

"One can hardly blame you . . . Diana."

He held out his arm, and I took it, allowing him to lead me over to where other couples were gathering at the start of the game.

I leaned close to him, keeping my voice low. "Do you know . . . ?"

"Appearances can be quite deceptive, don't you think?" he said.

"That is true."

"For example," he said, keeping his voice light and jovial, "your name is Diana, but I could swear I've known you before by another name."

He knew. This was his way of stating it without outright naming me.

"How are you with secrets, Lord Alosrin?" I asked.

He smiled softly. "There is nothing that would induce me to reveal what others must not know."

"Thank you again, sir," I said, giving him a curtsey as well.

"Any time, my lady." He waved to the game. "I see we will play Wellalee."

The game resembled a mini-golf course, Egyptian-style. Pyramids twice my height peppered the field, with smooth channels networking around them.

"How do we play?" I asked.

"First, we'll select a mallet. Each team will take turns driving the ball around the course. The first pair to reach the end wins."

"It sounds easy."

"It is, but that could be why they selected it for the first event. I assume they don't wish to overwhelm our kingdom's new arrivals."

We selected a mallet and ball and joined the other couples.

Axilya stood near the start of the course, holding what looked like a globe with a hole in the top. She beamed our way. "Hurry, hurry, now. Everyone, gather close. Each team will select a token that will show the order in which you will play."

Latarre chose ours, marked with the number one.

"First," he said. "A decided advantage."

I didn't care about winning. Who needed an estate if it didn't include Elion? My goal here was to make the time pass until the evening event, though I wasn't looking forward to my dance with Aillun. Perhaps the king would appear, and I'd get to provide the distraction before the music started.

"We start on the right," Latarre said, pointing in that direction. "Would you like to hit the ball first?"

"You go ahead."

He dropped it onto the ground and surveyed the course. "As you can see, the smooth passages weave back and forth among the pyramids. Do plan for distractions."

"Like what?" I asked.

A swooping sound rang out behind me, and he yanked on my arm, tugging me to the side.

The wings of an enormous black bird brushed my arm as it flew past, shrieking. It soared up over the course and settled on top of one of the pyramids.

Chapter 30
Raven

Latarre and I took turns driving the heavy ball around the course. Frankly, it wasn't as exciting as the game where we had to avoid the butterflies. That game ended in tragedy.

Hopefully, this one wouldn't.

I enjoyed being with Latarre. He made me laugh, something I needed to keep my stress from driving me out of my mind.

"Why are you here?" I asked him while we waited for others to take their turn.

A snake-like creature erupted from the sand at the base of the pyramid beside us, but I whacked it with the mallet, and it slunk back into the ground.

The sun beat down, relentlessly hot, and sweat crawled down my spine like a spider. I kept shifting my dress, trying to get rid of the itch.

"I came for the coronation," he said, his gaze shooting to Aillun. "I imagine everyone in the kingdom who can make it will be here for this . . . glorious event."

Anger burned through me, but I couldn't declare that the true king was still alive or that we had a plan to unseat Aillun, not in public like this.

"When is the coronation?" I asked, hoping it was far enough away we could prevent it. If everyone showed up, we could hold a party to celebrate King Khaidill's ongoing rule instead.

"Day after tomorrow," Latarre said, taking the mallet and shooting the ball around a curve.

So soon. This should give us enough time, assuming things went as expected tonight at the ball. If that didn't work, and none of us had been unveiled, we could regroup and try something different.

A centaur stomped through the course, and a few of the women shrieked before the beast galloped across the back lawn and entered the forest.

"You mustn't worry," he said kindly, his fingers gripping my shoulder. "Everything will work out."

I was doing my best to maintain my belief it would.

"Your turn," Latarre said, handing me the mallet. "Hit it extra hard. I bet it will travel the entire length of the course."

I laughed. "If it's anything like my last hits, it'll waggle about ten feet before coming to a stop. If we win today, it'll be because you're focused on the game, not through my efforts."

"Winning isn't always about ending first."

"True. It also comes from enjoying the game."

"Exactly," he said with a smile.

I hit the ball, crowing and hopping around when it scooted all the way to the end of this stretch, plunking against the farthest wall and rolling backward before coming to a stop.

"That'll help us maintain the lead," I said with a grin.

"It will." He studied my face. "You're an amazing person. Remember that. When things get tough, you're stronger than you believe."

"My life hasn't always been easy." I explained about my mom dying, and I could tell he felt bad for me by the sorrow in his eyes.

"And your little sister?"

"She's with my cousin. I'd started to hope I could . . ."

"Bring her here?"

"At first. While I'm sure she'd enjoy the magic and the colorful plants and odd creatures—the ones that don't try to kill, that is—I'm not sure this is the best place for her. She's a child. She has her whole life ahead of her." It shouldn't be bogged down by curses and evil fae determined to rule the kingdom.

"You changed your mind, then?"

"Yes." I sighed. "And that makes my heart clench because I want to be with her. She can't come here, and I'm not going back there. I . . ."

"You love someone from this realm."

"And he loves me."

"As he should," he said fiercely before releasing a low chuckle. "Excuse me for speaking so strongly. You are free to love whomever you please, but you're a nice person, and I want you to be happy."

"Thank you." I handed him the mallet. "It's your turn."

Once we'd rounded the next bend, we'd be hidden from those watching, Aillun especially. My spine would be able to ease, and I wouldn't feel like twitching.

He acted like he watched everyone play, but his gaze kept landing on me, containing a strange mix of puzzlement and irritation. His hand rested on a rail surrounding the course, and his finger kept tapping. Impatience or a nervous tic?

The weight of his attention made me drag my feet. It also made my flesh crawl. I couldn't tell if he knew who I was or if he was just plain old hot for Diana. Both thoughts spooked me.

I still hadn't seen Erleene or Follen, and that made me antsy as well, although a number of elf staff worked to prepare a meal for us beyond the game course. They could be busy in the kitchens.

Everything seemed to be going okay, but a feeling of doom persisted.

"As for the coronation," Latarre said once we'd rounded the bend and were alone. "I'd hoped..."

"What?"

He kept his voice low. "I really should not say this."

"It's me," I said. "You can share anything." Tension spiraled through me. I fingered the small blue stone encircled with silver wire he'd given me.

His gaze followed as I slid it back and forth along the chain. "I'm glad you still wear it."

"You told me to."

"That isn't enough of a reason."

It made me feel closer to him, though I had no idea why I needed that feeling. He was a stranger, someone who'd helped me when creatures nearly killed me in the inner realm.

He'd told me to call him when I was in great need. That time had not come, and if I was lucky, it never would.

"Are you able to break curses?" I asked.

"Not often," he said with a chuckle.

My shoulders slumped. So much for asking him to help Elion.

A cluster of hand-sized spiders slid down a pyramid and crawled along the side of the channel. I shuddered but couldn't even focus on something as scary as that. They scampered behind us and women gasped and bit off shrieks combined with laughter.

"Some suggest killing the person who laid the curse will end it," he said softly, frowning toward the spiders.

Elion told me he'd tried to kill Maverna, many times, and I was sure he wasn't the first one eager to end her life. How could a person with as little magic as I do something the fae couldn't?

Latarre lobbed the ball hard, and it coasted all the way to the end of this row. All I'd need to do was hit it hard enough to make it swirl around the loop at the end and start down the next channel. At about halfway through the course, we remained in the lead.

Perhaps I'd win the estate after all. I could gift it to Wren, who was paying more attention to her partner than the game. The guy she liked was doing the same thing, and that put them in last place.

"What were you about to say about the coronation?" I asked when we waited for others to take their turn.

He leaned close. "I hoped he'd be deposed by now."

"You and me both. No one seems to be willing to take on the challenge."

"Those who do will eventually succeed."

"That's good to hear," I said cheerfully, my mood lifting.

It was our turn again, and I lobbed the ball. For some reason, it deviated off the course, spinning up into the air and ricocheting back toward me.

Yelping, I ducked, and the ball shot past me, picking up speed. It hit the side of a pyramid and deflected upward, soaring through the sky before plunging back toward the ground.

Someone cried out in pain, and a guy bellowed in dismay.

Latarre and I ran back through the course.

When I rounded the final bend, I came to a shuddering stop.

"What have you done?" the fae guy who liked Wren shouted, rushing at me with his hands raised. "You hit her. She's not breathing!"

"That will be enough," Axilya shouted, stepping between us. "This is a terrible accident. Nothing else."

My lungs aflame, I raced around her with Latarre on my heels.

Wren lay on the ground, unmoving, with the mangled ball lying beside her.

Chapter 31
Elion

My father and the strange woman kept kissing. Their moans deepened.

I stared at my hands. She wasn't my mother. He was cheating on her. He was cheating on us. Why?

Their hands grew feverish, and it was clear they thought they were alone, that they could do whatever they wanted without anyone finding out. My mother sat in the parlor, stitching. My sister had probably joined her, groaning when Mother asked her to play some music or quizzed her about what we'd done together. None of the staff wandered this far into the forest.

I was grateful I'd taken Truella back and waited until she'd entered the castle. At least she didn't have to witness this.

My father growled. "Yes," he cried as she kissed his chest.

Bile surged up into my mouth, but I swallowed it back down, like I'd swallow what I'd seen here today.

Forget about it. Toss it in with the rest of the refuse littering my life.

I couldn't tell Mother, and Truella had never been my confidant, not that she'd understand.

No one but me would ever know.

"You only want me," the woman said with high-pitched urgency. "Tell me."

"I only want you."

"You'll be with no one but me."

"No one."

I didn't like how deadened his voice sounded. This didn't make sense. How could he promise another woman something he should only give to my mother?

I wasn't naïve. The staff gossiped, and it was easy to overhear about this person joining that one in the closet or tumbling onto a bed in an unused room.

It was clear this wasn't the first time they'd been together.

They tugged at each other's clothing, tearing them away, and their sighs and groans grew louder, grating across my flesh like a dull blade. Dull, perhaps, but it sliced deeply, severing something vital inside me.

When they dropped to their knees in the deep grass and then to the ground, still tearing at each other's clothing, I turned away, unable to bear witness to this any longer. If I could creep away, I would, but I feared they'd hear me.

I had to try. I turned and started crawling, remaining in the deep grass. My lungs ached, and tears stung my eyes. Reality had shoved aside my dreams, and I was sure

I'd never be able to come here again. I would never pretend I was a soldier again. Dreams were for little ones, not someone who'd seen . . . this.

A stick snapped beneath my knee, and I stopped moving, my pulse thumping heavily in my throat.

"What was that?" the woman asked, not as far gone with my father as I'd hoped.

"Nothing," he said with a laugh. "Who'd see us here?"

"Your wife," she hissed.

"She's busy at the castle, puttering or giving the staff orders."

The woman snapped her teeth together. "She'll be angry if she finds out."

"What will she do?"

"Divorce you. Tell the kingdom about us."

"She won't," he said with complete confidence. "She wouldn't dare. Come now, lay back in the grass and let me pleasure you."

My belly twisted into a knot and rage flashed through me, making me grip the grass tight enough to rip it partway from the ground. I hated him in that instant as much as I hated her. How dare he slash through the complacent life I'd been lulled into?

"Why wouldn't she divorce you?" the woman asked, her low laughter breaking through her words.

"Because she needs my wealth. She needs me."

"You could leave her and give her a stipend," the woman said. "Once you married, it became your wealth. Then we could be together."

"You get ahead of yourself," my father said, his anger clear.

"You want me. You want to be with me." Desperation lifted the woman's voice.

"And I *am* with you, am I not?" he said.

"You won't leave her, will you?" she barked. "Not ever."

I felt the world still around me and knew in that moment that something huge was about to happen.

"No, I will not," he said calmly. "She brings a title my father denied his second son. Decent estates, despite the needed repairs. And respect."

"I could give you respect."

He snorted. "You have no title to offer. No estates."

"You . . ." The grass rustled as if she moved through it quickly. I didn't look up, but I suspected she was tugging on her clothing, blocking her body from his view. "How dare you? I loved you. I believed in you."

"Come now," my father said. "We can still have fun."

I dared a peek and found him sitting on the ground, looking up at her. He wore nothing, and there wasn't a swear word large and nasty enough that would define how horrible a person he'd become in my eyes.

Become? No, I suspected this was the true father I'd loved. The one I'd looked up to but no longer would.

With her back to me, the woman lifted her clutch and pulled something from it. It gleamed in the sunlight.

"What are you doing?" Panic filled my father's eyes as he scrambled away from her, his pale, pasty flesh pinkened from the sunlight.

"You have wronged me. Scorned me," she intoned. Magic swirled around her as she cast a spell, one that would haunt him for a lifetime. "No one in your family will find true love. This I swear. You and yours are doomed!"

She rushed toward my father and brought the knife down hard, hitting his throat. While he smacked her arms and flailed, she continued slashing.

Even when he lay slumped on the ground, she didn't stop. She bent over and delivered one blow after another until only a pulpy mass stared up at her blankly.

Straightening, her cackle rang out.

Tears streamed down my face, and it was all I could do not to sob like a little kid.

Blood sheathed her arms. My *father's* blood. It dripped off her fingers. The knife. It melted into the ground.

I dragged my gaze up to the woman's face. She stared right at me.

My heart froze.

A sweep of her hand, and magic . . .

Chapter 32
Raven

Wren lay on the ground. Dead from the blow of the ball against her forehead, where a shadowy bruise had formed.

The other women shrieked. Danica turned and threw up, her breakfast splattering her legs.

"I . . ." I realized I still clutched our mallet. I stared down at it before tossing it away. "I didn't do it. I didn't kill her!"

I peered around wildly. Should I run?

"It was an accident," Axilya cried, rushing to me. She wrapped her arms around me. "Diana, dear. Never fear. You did not cause this. Of course, no one believes you would harm Wren."

"Never," Aillun cried, and even he looked shook. He squinted at the pyramid. "Explain what happened."

"I hit the ball to shoot it around the corner, but it deviated," I said. "It hit a pyramid, shot up into the sky, then came down fast."

"You have no magic to cause such a thing to happen," he said, studying my face.

"How could I?" My hands shook, and it was all I could do to remember I was still Diana and not Raven. "I'm human."

"Poor Wren," Danica cried, dropping down beside the dead woman, her hands fluttering. "She . . ." Her gaze sought the fae guy who had been so enthralled by Wren.

He'd collapsed on the ground on the opposite side of her, his hand stroking her cheek. "She was here. She was alive. I . . . She was everything to me."

Axilya left me and stooped down beside him to give him a hug. "I am sorry, Zyan. Truly sorry. It was a terrible accident."

"It was," Aillun said dully.

My heart pinched for Wren, and despite knowing I hadn't done anything wrong, I still felt guilty.

"There isn't anything you could've done differently," Latarre said in a low voice behind me. "You are not at fault."

I turned, my gaze seeking his, and I was grateful when I only found sympathy there.

"I didn't *make* the ball shoot up over the pyramid," I blurted out. I hadn't hit it any harder than all the other times. If anything, I'd gone softer with that hit, since I only needed to nudge it around the bend.

Reaching for the charm Elion gave me, I clutched it. I needed him now more than ever. So much. His arms around me, his reassuring touch.

Soon, I promised. *Soon.*

Please.

"I will escort you to your room," Aillun said, taking my arm and tugging me away from Latarre.

"I don't . . ." Pulling out of his grasp, I backed up until I ran into Latarre.

Latarre's hand dropped onto my shoulder. "She's flustered. Upset about what just happened. I think she needs to rest."

"I can get to my room on my own," I said as kindly as possible.

"Do you refuse me?" Aillun said in a low tone. Fury flashed across his face, and he snapped a finger toward me.

A shudder ripped through me, but I didn't know why.

"Oh, um . . ." Why were we arguing about something like this? Who cared how I made it to my room?

All I kept picturing was what had just happened. Wren. The poor fae guy whose dreams were shattered.

Guards appeared and nudged him away from her. A pop, and Wren's body disappeared.

"What did they do with her?" I asked.

"She will be sent back to her family," Axilya said with tears in her eyes. "Such a sweet woman. I had such high hopes for her and Zyan." Her gaze fell on Aillun. "I'm sure you have much to do. The humans will be worried. Two tragedies in such a short time are almost too much for us to bear."

Another accident? I suspected the killer had struck again.

I started to shout this out, but Latarre's hand tapped my shoulder. I peered up at him, and he gave me a tiny shake of his head.

All right. We'd talk about this later.

"The ball can't go on," I said. "How could anyone dance?"

"It must," Axilya said. "It is vital we solidify the truce."

How could a truce hold when women kept being murdered? I wanted to scream the words, to make someone listen.

"Such a terrible accident," Aillun said, turning away. For that, at least, I could be grateful. "You are correct, Axilya. I have a lot to do. First, I will notify the authorities in the human world, then I will send the poor woman's body home."

My throat tightened, and tears erupted from my eyes.

"Come," Axilya said, putting her arm around me, easing me away from Latarre. "I'll walk with you to your room."

Latarre nodded. "I will remove the game."

"Thank you," she said, her concerned gaze seeking mine. As we left the others, she lowered her voice. "You are not responsible, Diana. Please believe me. It was an accident. A horrible, sad accident."

"Thank you for being here for me," I said.

"Any time. Yes, this is my role as guardian, but I care. Please know this."

Warmth suffused me, and I nodded. "I can tell you do."

She took me to my room and waited until one of the elf staff arrived to be with me. Frankly, I wanted to be alone, but even in this, I had to remain Diana.

As for the ball, I had no way of getting word to the others. This left me with no choice but to attend the event. We had to complete the plan.

The elf lady chattered, drawing a bath she said would soothe me, and even offering to send a drink that would take away my tension.

"Just the bath," I said, needing my wits about me.

"Very well." She tugged a pale pink gown from the wardrobe and held it out, scrutinizing it. From her cheery tone of voice, I assumed she hadn't yet heard about Wren. But word would spread fast throughout the castle. "I believe this dress will look lovely on you tonight." A soft smile fluttered across her face. "Have any of the fae gentlemen caught your eye yet?"

Only Elion. There was no one for me but him.

"Not so far," I said.

"There will be more here tonight," she said, laying the gown on the bed and smoothing the fabric. "I'll do your hair, and King Aillun specifically told me he would send jewelry for you to wear to the event."

I had a feeling he'd be upset if I refused to wear it, though I'd rip it off the second everything was over.

"That's nice of him."

She chuckled, though kindly. "I believe you have caught the king's eye."

That was the last thing I'd ever wanted to happen.

I stripped and stepped into the tub, sinking down

until the water covered my shoulders. My teeth wouldn't stop chattering, and my skin crawled with fear.

Had it been an accident or had someone murdered Wren? Even now, I couldn't believe what had happened.

The ball had roared toward my head. Whenever I closed my eyes, I saw it. When I ducked, it hit the pyramid and deflected upward.

Had someone tried to kill *me*?

Or Diana, I supposed.

Unless someone other than Latarre knew I was Diana in disguise.

Despite the heat of the water, I couldn't warm up. My teeth rattled together, and my hands wouldn't stop shaking. I bathed quickly and climbed out of the tub.

The elf woman helped me dry off and dress in a nightie.

"I'm not going to bed," I protested weakly.

She led me over to the satin-covered surface. "Lie down. I promise, if you sleep, you'll feel much better when you wake. I *am* going to send that drink." She shook her finger in my face, but only kindness filled her eyes. "Drink it. Sleep. I'll wake you in plenty of time to get ready for the ball."

There would be no harm in doing as she asked.

I slipped beneath the covers and stretched out. The bed was enormous. I didn't disturb the gown lying at the foot of it.

While the elf woman tidied the room, a drink appeared on the bedside table.

I sat up and lifted it, determined to drink it all and let

whatever spell she'd concocted soothe me. I'd barely slept the night before, consumed with worry for Elion and the others. This trauma sure hadn't helped. A little nap would help keep me alert later for the most vital part of our plan.

But when I lifted the drink to my lips, the elf dashed across the room.

She knocked the glass from my hand, and it soared into the wall. Shattering with a loud clang, it oozed across the surface. Liquid dripped, burning the paint off like acid.

"I did not call for that drink," she said sharply, her gaze focused on the wall that continued to melt. "I do not understand. Who here would send you poison?"

Chapter 33
Raven

I gaped at the wall. "Someone tried to kill me."

"I . . ." The elf backed away from the bed, her gaze flying around the room. "I will send guards. Remain here." A pop, and she disappeared.

Pounding began on my door not long after. By then, I'd climbed from the bed and dressed in regular clothing. I stood by the window, wondering if I could remain within the castle long enough for the ball.

"Let me in, Diana," Aillun bellowed, banging some more.

Go away, I wanted to shout, but he was the king. I strode over to the door and opened it, but when he started to step inside, I nudged past him to stand in the hall. His guards stared at me while Aillun rummaged around in my room.

He came out, and the guards backed away, two on each side to provide Aillun protection.

"I removed the offending items," he said.

I wished I could read his eyes, because I swore a sly tint shot through them before he erected a mask.

He seemed to be enamored with Diana, though, making it hard to believe he'd try to kill her. But someone was doing this.

This was just another reason to ensure the king retook his throne. He would not allow this to continue.

However, Ivaran had bought into the accident story with the first group of women. I'd heard nothing from him since to convince me he'd view what happened to Wren as murder.

But someone trying to poison me? He'd believe that.

"You are uninjured?" Aillun said, his gaze skimming down my front. When he lifted his eyes, I didn't miss the subtle leer.

"I'm fine," I said.

"Good," he barked. He nudged his head to the guards on his right. "Remain here with Diana. Ensure she is safe." He gripped my arms a little too tight. "They will watch over you until you can join me at the ball."

"How can we hold a ball now?"

"Accidents happen. You know this," he said with a scowl. "I will not postpone this event. Tonight, I plan to announce the time and place of my coronation. Soon, I will rule forever."

Not if we could stop it from happening. "I heard your coronation was scheduled for day after tomorrow."

"Who told you that?"

I frowned and shrugged. "I can't remember."

"This is a mere rumor. It is not official." He flashed

me a smile, his good mood restored. "Remember, you said you would dance with me first." After running his oily gaze down my front, he strode away, gesturing for two of his guardsmen to follow.

The elf servant appeared in the doorway and urged me to enter the room.

Aillun had eliminated the stain and the broken glass.

Had he also eliminated the evidence? He seemed to still believe I was Diana, so why would he try to harm her?

I couldn't figure this out. Once I was back with my friends, and I'd shared what happened within the castle and grounds, they'd have ideas for what we should do next.

Lying down was not an option. I paced the room while the elf woman watched. I assumed she'd been sent back to provide guard duty inside the bedroom.

Finally, it was time to get ready for the ball.

The servant helped me dress, then plunked me in a chair so she could fix my hair. She took care of my face with magic.

"Here is the jewelry Aillun sent," she said, lifting a case off the bureau and opening the top to reveal a necklace and earrings that were so encrusted with sparkly stones I wanted to shield my eyes from the glare.

"Lovely," I said dully. I had a bad feeling about this but couldn't think of a way to get out of it. I was a ball tumbling down a mountainside, unable to slow my fall.

"Aren't they gorgeous? I believe they were crafted by the crown's very own troll jeweler." She tilted the velvet-lined box, and the necklace gleamed in the light. "She does amazing work and is in high demand."

"I can see why."

She secured the necklace around my throat, then frowned, flipping the charm from Elion and the blue stone from Latarre I still wore. "You should remove this. It's interfering with the beauty of the jewels."

"I don't want to," I said.

Her frown deepened. "I think you should." She started to reach for the clasp, but I stilled her hand.

"Leave them alone." I backed away from her. "You're not touching them."

Her huff rang out. "All right. Do not complain if Aillun scowls. You will bring his displeasure on yourself."

"I'll deal with King Aillun," I said pertly, still clutching the charm and the stone.

"Very well." She dipped forward in a very shallow bow. "If you don't need anything else, I will return to my regular duties."

"Thank you for helping me get ready."

"You are welcome." Rather than disappear, she strode through the door, greeting the guards as she shut the panel behind her.

It looked like it was time to head to the ball. I sucked in a breath and released it, then did it again, but nothing was going to still my heart until this was over—and over in the way we'd planned it.

Soon, I'd see Elion. The king would storm into the room and gasps would ring out. I'd create a diversion, but

I'd also watch Aillun, because I was eager to see his downfall. He'd tried to kill the man he believed was his father. He deserved whatever came after the confrontation.

How would Ivaran punish Aillun? It appeared I was about to find out.

I left the room, and the guards followed me down the stairs and along the south hallway to the enormous ballroom.

I'd barely stepped inside when Aillun stomped over to me.

"You will dance with me," he said, latching onto my hand.

It was not a request.

I didn't like the idea of being close to him, but I couldn't see a way out of a dance. At least I didn't have to hang out with him long after that. I could lurk along the wall and sip a drink, waiting until Erleene and Follen showed up to give me the cue.

Then all hell would break loose, and I could shrug off the façade of Diana.

"I'd be delighted to dance with you, King Aillun," I said, pushing for a smile that did not come easy.

He took me into his arms and swept me around the room to the music crafted by what looked like a big bouquet of flowers. They dipped and swayed, and, when we passed, I spied tiny instruments among their petals and stems.

"I hope you are feeling better after the afternoon's mishap," he said, staring down at me.

My flesh crawled where his hand spanned my lower back. "Yes."

How could I politely leave him on the ballroom floor?

The doors leading to the patio door banged open. Was it time for the distraction?

I strained to see past Aillun as gasps rang out in the room. This must be it. Yay. It would soon be over.

But my heart stalled when I saw Diana—a bedraggled Diana—stagger into the room from the patio.

She spied Aillun and released a thready cry. She stumbled over to where we'd stopped dancing. Collapsing at his feet, she reached up and clung to his legs.

Whimpering, she pretty much tried to climb his leg. Why?

His smirk gave him away.

He'd lured her. All the times I felt something subtle drift over me, it had been Aillun trying to lure "Diana" into his arms.

Aillun shook her off. She remained on the floor, sobbing.

"You." He latched onto my arms and shook me. He waved for guards to help Diana, who crawled after him as Aillun dragged me from the room. "Come with me."

It wasn't a request, and the steel in his eyes told me I was in deep shit.

"Of course, King Aillun," I said. Was now a good time to provide a distraction? Erleene or Follen were supposed to give me the signal, and if there was any time to do it, it was now. But I didn't see them or the king anywhere.

He marched me to a door on the back wall of the ballroom.

Speculation rang out in the room, and whispers followed us as he hauled me through the crowd.

I tried to think of a plan to get away. The gig was up, and I was about to be grounded.

Wrenching backward, I slipped from his grip, but he grabbed the back of my dress before I could take one step.

He took me to a small room beyond the ballroom, where he pressed me against a wall.

His hand wrapped around my throat, tightening.

"Where is my father, Raven?" he growled.

Chapter 34
Elion

I woke, unsure where I was and what had happened.

A memory niggled at the back of my mind, but I couldn't remember what it was. I shook it off. I was locked in a cell in the dungeon and escaping needed to be my focus.

When I shifted on the hard surface—the stone floor?—my groan ripped from my throat.

"Elion," Follen hissed. "Elion?"

I propped myself up on my palms and peered around, noting nothing but the time had changed. When Aillun threw me against the wall, I must've been knocked unconscious.

"Are you all right?" Follen asked, clinging to the bars in the cell opposite mine.

"I woke up, so that's good." Rubbing the back of my head, I winced. I had a big bump, but the skin's surface wasn't broken.

"You've been unconscious for a very long time."

"How long?"

"All night," he said. "It is late afternoon. I am surprised you woke. You were so still. I thought..."

That Aillun had done what Maverna was determined to do herself. End my life.

"The ball," I said. "We have to get out of here and find the king."

"I have tried everything," Follen moaned. "My power is blocked, and Erleene has not returned. I am truly worried. I fear our plan is going to fail."

Raven would attend the ball tonight. She'd expect a cue from us to provide a distraction. What would she do if we didn't arrive?

Again, I felt like there was something I needed to remember, but each time I tried to grasp the memory, it slipped from my mind's fingers. I shrugged it off. If it was important, it would come to me.

I scrubbed my face with my palms, dragging my fingers across the top of my head. With a groan, I rose to my feet, staggering before righting myself with a palm braced on the wall. A few steps put me at the bunk, and I dropped onto it, leaning back against the wall with my head spinning.

When I shot magic out at the cell door, it snapped back to bite me. I hissed but kept trying.

"The same happens to me," Follen said sadly. "No one ever escapes the dungeon."

Our magic was blocked, keeping us from escaping, but would simple spells work?

I gathered a bit of power and crafted a healing spell,

sending it to my head, relieved when it took, and the pain lessened.

Follen would do whatever he could, but like me, he was stuck here while things progressed without us. Would the king be able to handle this himself? Follen and I were supposed to distract the guards to give him time to enter the ballroom. Erleene and Follen would cue Raven to provide the distraction before joining the king to give him magical cover.

"Any ideas for how we can get out of here?" I growled, unwilling to sit on the bunk while my friends were in danger. "Could we combine magic again to open one of the locks?"

"We can try. Send me some. My injuries have healed."

I gathered what I could and shot it to Follen, sad to see I could collect so little, but that was the point of blocks. They'd keep us from touching all of it if they could, but no one had figured out how to do that yet.

His eyes closed; his fists tightened at his sides. Strain creased his face.

I sensed more than saw him send the magic at the door.

His shoulders slumped as what little he'd consolidated drained away, but hope filled his eyes as he yanked on the door.

It remained locked.

His growl rang out, combining with mine.

"You try," he said, tugging in power. He gave it to me, but I couldn't open my door either.

ICE LORD'S FATE

"We're stuck here," I said, hating feeling this useless.

Without me and Follen, I couldn't see how our plan would go well.

"We tried," he said. "And we will keep trying. One of these times, it might work."

At least it was something we could do.

Time ticked along as if it grabbed onto me and dragged me across the stone floor. Each bump and jar created a wound that would never heal. I watched a spider work on its web above me, and when a fly buzzed near, it caught it.

That was me, the fly caught in Aillun's web. He'd do the same as the spider, wrap me up and, later, eat me. Or he'd leave me in the dungeon until my curse ran out and claimed me. He didn't have to do anything to kill me.

Worry for Raven consumed me. I rose and paced, thinking about the king. Erleene. And examining every bit of the walls and floor, prying at stones to see if any would loosen. Magic encased this part of the dungeon, too, and nothing shifted.

"It is evening," Follen finally said, peering up at the thin slice of window mounted near the ceiling. "The moon rises, and the ball must be starting." With a sigh, he lowered himself onto his bunk.

We shot light magic at our doors repeatedly, but each attempt drained us further, and we were gaining nothing.

"How did it come to this?" Despair filled Follen's voice. "I thought we could do this, that we could defeat Aillun and put the king back in his rightful place. Good should always triumph over evil."

Only in fairytales.

"I'm sorry I involved you in this," I said.

He sat up on his bunk, staring at me with great sympathy. "How could I do anything less? Can you see me accepting Aillun's rule? I would fight his attempt to steal the throne."

"You're locked in a dungeon because of me."

"I do this for you, yes, but for the entire kingdom. For my fellow elves and the fae. None of us will fare well under Aillun's rule."

Bangs rang out from the stairwell, and we both looked that way. Was Aillun returning? I didn't have the strength to fight him, though I'd try.

The door was thrust open, and three guards strode down the hallway between the cells. They stopped and studied Follen before turning to me.

"I've been told to take you into the woods," one guard said. His eyes didn't meet mine, spelling trouble.

My guts sank, and I scrambled to gather the wisps of power I was permitted, knowing it would never be enough, but unable to come up with a better plan.

Follen watched me, his face filled with quiet desperation. His fingers kept snapping toward the guards, and they flinched, no doubt feeling his magic, but it wasn't strong enough to give them anything more than the sting of a bite.

"I have no need to walk in the woods," I said.

"I'm sorry," was all the guard could say. "Come with me quietly, or I'll have to force you." He dropped his voice to a whisper. "Don't make this harder. You are a fellow fae lord, but I am compelled to do as the king asks."

"You plan to kill me, and you're asking me to cooperate?" I said with a snort.

"I have no choice. King Aillun rules, and we obey." He opened my cell door and stepped inside.

I stood and faced them with my head held high. Cooperating now did not mean I wouldn't use this opportunity to escape.

With my eyes, I told Follen that I'd come back for him. His eyes told me he was worried I wouldn't be given the chance.

A flick of the guard's hand, magical bindings looped around my wrists and ankles, securing my hands tightly together. They gave my feet just enough freedom to take short, shuffling steps.

Guards grabbed my arms and hustled me from the cell.

My gaze met Follen's as I passed.

"Go in peace, my friend," he said.

Chapter 35
Raven

"Where is the king?" Aillun bellowed, his spittle smacking my face.

"Excuse me," Latarre said from the doorway. "I was looking for the bathroom?"

Aillun blinked at him, frowning.

I jerked my knee up, scoring big time with a hit on his balls.

He groaned and released me, bending forward and cupping himself.

I bolted into the ballroom with Latarre.

The other women descended, fluttering around us, and asking all kinds of questions. Guards stormed in our direction.

I sensed more than felt spells hitting me, deflected by the charm Elion had given me. Once again, I was grateful to have it.

Latarre's face tightened, and he swirled his hand in the air to block the spells attacking him.

"What's happening?" Axilya cried out, rushing over to me. She looked from me to the real Diana still sitting on the floor and backed away, her eyes widening. "We have an imposter in our midst. Which of you is the *real* Diana? Where is the king? He must fix this."

The king would get on it right away, assuming he could walk. I wasn't going to hang around here to find out. I could no longer be a part of our plan. Escape had become my priority.

I wrenched away from the Axilya's grasping hands and ran for the hall with Latarre, slamming aside a guard when he tried to block our way through the door.

"Where can we hide?" I asked, pausing in the hall.

Latarre's frantic gaze met mine. "I'm not sure."

Aillun would do anything to find us.

"Can you take us to the inner realm?" I asked.

"Not from inside the castle. Aillun has done something to block access."

It was time to flee into the woods, then.

Magical beams slammed into the wall beside my head, making me duck.

Latarre gripped my arm. "Run. I'll hold them back."

"What about you?" The thought of him getting hurt made my chest tighten.

His grim smile met mine. "Don't worry about me. I've got a few tricks up my sleeve."

Uncertainty filled me, but when another blast of magic smacked into me, knocking me back against the wall, though not causing damage due to my charm, I had no choice.

"Find me," I said, studying his face as if it was the last time I'd see him.

He nodded and pinched his eyes closed for a second. His body wavered before disappearing. Had he left?

But when guards rushed toward me, they jerked to a stop and went flying backward, hitting the far wall.

Ah, he was invisible, a neat trick I'd love to learn.

Because I knew he had a chance, I ran, eventually finding myself in the foyer. Two guards flanked the door. They stared at me, probably wondering why one of the human women had decided to go for a jog while dressed in a ballgown.

Aillun would expect me to flee outside, and frankly, that was where I wanted to go. There were plenty of places to hide in the forest.

The guards would tell Aillun where I went, so I bolted out the front door. Instead of running down the stairs and around the building, I crept to the left and carefully peered into the front parlor. Seeing no one inside, I lifted the window and slipped into the room.

Shouts rang out in the foyer, and stomps echoed outside on the front balcony.

I hurried across the room to the opposite side, where a door led to another room. As long as no one lurked in the other rooms, I could continue through the castle.

But I didn't hold much hope that all of them would be empty.

Then I remembered the tunnel Koko had used. Did anyone else know about it?

I made my way in that direction, hiding behind doors whenever someone stomped past in the outer hall.

Through the window, I spied guards searching the grounds. Shouts rang out here and there. The odds of my remaining free for long were fading fast.

After peeking out and ensuring the hall was empty, I raced down it, exiting into the room where Koko had taken me. I scurried to the wall, stooping in the corner where Koko had revealed a secret passage.

I pressed on that section, but nothing happened. My growl echoed around me. He must've used magic to open it, and I was fresh out of magic. Except . . .

With my eyes closed, I sought the bit of power I'd discovered when we cast the spell to create our disguises. When I saw the magic, I tried to grab it, but it slipped through my fingers like silk threads. The magic bound together again, and I reached for it, only to lose it again.

Damn you, I thought, and the mass of magic stopped spinning. Was it listening to me? The assumption felt silly, but who knew when it came to magic?

"Come here," I whispered.

It ebbed and flowed, oozing in my direction. Every color of the rainbow was contained within it, and if I had time, I'd sit back and stare at it. It mesmerized me. Where had it come from? Had it been with me all this time, but I just hadn't seen it?

The why and where of this didn't matter. I needed to find a way to harness it and make it do my bidding.

Yelling at it wasn't working, so I tried coaxing, holding out my hand like I would to a scared pup.

"Come closer, little one," I whispered, feeling stupid.

But the oozing magic glided toward me before stopping. Leave it to me to have shy magic.

"Come on," I said, struggling to remain patient. "Jump into my arms and let me . . ." Use you. "We can play." That sounded better.

The magic came closer. When I called it again, it slid nearer. Soon, I could grab onto it and coax it to do what it could to help me.

"I want to open the panel," I said, as if the magic would understand me. "Aillun is looking for me, and it's the only place I can think of to hide."

The magic soared toward me, coming to rest in my mind's open palms.

That simple, huh?

How did I use it? I'd essentially given it to the Erleene, and when I needed it to produce claws, nothing happened. They popped out of my fingertips all on their own. Fear had been a driving factor, and panic swirled through me now. But I didn't need claws. I needed to open the tiny door.

This power was mine. I'd have to figure it out someday, but there wasn't time for training.

I tossed it at the wall, and it went willingly, slamming against the surface before rebounding back into me, though now a smaller mass and with dimmer colors.

How did it replenish itself? I'd ask Elion if—no, *when* —I saw him again.

For now, I assumed it either needed to rest or it would take from me to grow again.

At least I didn't feel tired.

I placed both palms on the wall. A push, and it creaked inward, creating a doorway. I crawled through, and the panel shut behind me.

I'd been here before, but it was just as creepy now as it was then.

Crawling, I continued down the steep slope that took me deep beneath the main floors of the castle. My eyes slowly adjusted to the darkness, making it easier to pick up the cobwebs lining the ceiling.

Lovely.

Shivering, I continued moving along the smooth stone floor, taking in the walls curving up to the low ceiling made of big rock slabs. When I could, I rose to a crouch and hurried, sensing time mattered.

Like before, subtle scrapes echoed from ahead. My heart slammed against my ribcage, and my palms grew sweaty. I moved slowly and carefully, not wanting anyone to hear me.

Soft light bloomed ahead, and I went faster, almost running until the tunnel ended, exiting out into the intersection with a long stone wall opposite of where I stood. Passages extended to my left and right. The door to the cell where I'd found the king was partway open. When I nudged it inward farther, it groaned, and I found the room empty.

I didn't want to go back the way I'd come. There must be a way out of this level somewhere.

I hurried to my right but found the door at the end of the hall locked. The one on the left end of the passageway opened, and after pausing to listen and hearing nothing, I stepped out into a dungeon.

"Ah, there you are," Erleene said, waving for me to come closer. She stood in front of a cell, and a flick of her hand made the door creak open.

Follen rushed out into the hall, and I realized neither of them wore their disguises any longer.

"Am I still Diana?" I asked.

She nodded. "The spell will wear off by tomorrow. We ended ours when it was clear Aillun had discovered who we are."

"He knows I'm Raven," I said.

"All right then." She pinched her eyes shut, and I felt her magic float across me like a cool mist. My hands morphed back into my own, and when I touched my face, it felt familiar. I no longer looked like Diana.

"We need to leave," Erleene said. "We'll find the king and form a new plan."

"Not without Elion," I said. "I have to find him." I could take the same passage and sneak through the castle. He was here somewhere, and I'd track him down.

"We must hurry," Follen said. "At Aillun's command, the guards have taken Elion into the woods." His solemn gaze met mine. "They are going to kill him."

Chapter 36
Elion

One spell, and my magic froze as if a wall of ice separated me from it.

"That'll make you behave," a guard said with a sneer.

Four guards hustled me from the dungeon, up a few flights of stairs, and out through the back entrance of the castle.

With my magical binds, I couldn't run. But . . .

I shifted into my wolf form, but I only made it two padded steps before the bindings tightened, biting past my fur and into my flesh. Tumbling forward, I slammed against the ground.

I'd hoped the magic would dissipate when I shifted, but that would be too easy.

Winded, I twisted back into my fae form.

"Don't try that again," a guard said, hauling me to my feet. He shoved me across the grass, keeping me from falling but making me half-run toward the woods.

"What are you going to do with me?" I asked, though

I knew. We weren't out for a walk, and we weren't going to pick flowers.

"You know I don't want to do this," he said. "But the king rules, and we obey."

The other guards watched us, though they remained a few paces behind. Far enough away to keep from overhearing?

I leaned close to the first. "King Ivaran lives."

"He is dead. You killed him," he said grimly. "This is why I'm happy to obey our new sire, Aillun."

"And what if you're wrong? What if King Ivaran does live? That means I didn't kill him and something else is going on."

He scowled, and I sensed I was getting nowhere, but I had to keep trying. If he softened, I could take advantage of the lull.

"I'll play along for a bit," he said. "Tell me what else is going on." He waved for the others to drop further behind.

We reached the edge of the forest and started down a path, weaving toward a big open meadow. I'd gone there sometimes to relax. Now it would be the spot of my death unless I could convince the guards to release me.

What would the other guards do if I convinced this one?

"Aillun tried to kill the king, and he blamed it on me," I said.

"He was King Ivaran's heir. Why would Aillun need to kill him? He'd inherit in due time."

"Do you think Aillun was patient enough to wait?"

The guard grumbled, his face scrunching. "He wouldn't kill his father."

"He doesn't know who his father is."

His eyes widening, the guard halted on the path. "You're crafting an amazing story, but I don't believe a word you're saying."

Now or never, right?

"I'm the king's true son. Aillun is Maverna's son, and she switched us at birth."

The guard burst into laughter. He grabbed onto my arm and shoved me. "Keep going. I'm enjoying this more than I should. You, the true son of the king? Switched at birth? What do you take me for, a fairy?"

Some called the fae fairies, but I didn't point that out.

"It's true. King Ivaran and I came here to confront Aillun, but he saw through our plan and captured me."

"You killed his father. That's why he captured you."

"Don't I deserve a trial, a public accusation with a chance to state my side of the story?" I asked.

His lips thinned. "That was before I saw the overwhelming evidence."

"And what evidence is that?"

"Aillun produced the cup the old king drank from. It had your markings all over it."

"Do you think he couldn't cast a spell to make it appear that way?"

I kept trying, though it was clear he didn't believe anything I was saying. Desperation grated down my spine. We'd stop walking soon. Would they kill me immediately or stake me to the ground and leave me for the beasts who hunted the woods?

I broke into a hobbling run but restrained. I didn't get far before he grabbed my arm.

"And that's why you're running. You know you're lying and that I see through it." He nodded decisively. "And that's why you need to die."

We reached a small meadow, and I scrambled to find some way to slow this down. I needed time to think, to find a way to get free.

They shoved me into the middle of the meadow.

The sun had crept above the horizon, and I had to wonder if this would be the last time I'd see the beauty of a new dawn. To think I might miss a chance to see Raven once more.

My wife. My love. My true mate.

Pain crashed through me. It wasn't supposed to end like this. I wanted the chance to break my spell, to spend my life with the woman I loved.

Aillun was stealing that from me, just like his mother.

They slammed me onto the ground on my back. As I'd assumed, they magically bound me to the surface with deeply placed stakes. I tried to pull my magic, but it remained walled away from me.

The guard I'd tried to convince stood over me. "This will teach you not to murder a king."

"We should kill him outright," one of the other guards said. "He doesn't deserve to live even one more moment." He pulled his blade and stooped down beside me.

But when he lifted his knife to plunge it into my chest, his face tightened.

Magic erupted in the meadow, hitting guards like laser beams from a human space movie. They fell, groaning while toppling over. None of them moved again.

Raven strode over to stand beside me, with Follen and Erleene crowding behind her.

She blew on her finger and gave me a grim smile. "That'll teach 'em to hurt the guy I love."

Chapter 37
Raven

Erleene made quick work of magicking away Elion's bindings, and he swept me up in his arms, spinning us as he kissed me. When he lowered my feet to the ground, my head spun, and I couldn't keep my smile off my face.

"Safe again," I said.

"For now."

"Has anyone seen the king?" Erleene asked.

"I was going to him when I was captured," Elion said. "Aillun saw through my magical disguise."

"Mine as well," Erleene said.

"I thought I'd fooled him with this." I fingered my charm. "But he was just playing with me." A shudder tore through me. I'd come very close to being captured.

"He suspects we're helping the king," Elion said. "He asked me where he was. But he doesn't know the final twist yet."

"The king didn't show up at the ball," I said. "Latarre helped me escape."

I hoped he was safe. Had he gotten away?

"Can you take us to the king through the inner realm?" I asked Erleene.

"Not all of you at once," she said.

"Go to the king and bring him here, then," Elion said.

A pop, and she disappeared, returning not long after with the king, who was also no longer disguised.

"I saw what happened from the balcony," he said to me. "And when the rest of you didn't arrive, I knew that was not the time for my confrontation. We need to do something different, something Aillun won't suspect is a trap." He looked around at us. "Ideas?"

"We need to hit Aillun hard enough to knock him out for good." I peered around at my friends. "What about crashing his coronation?"

A tic thrummed on the king's temple, and a growl ripped through him. "When is this scheduled?"

"Tomorrow," I said.

"What time?"

"He was going to announce it at the ball, but I'm sure one of us could find out from the staff. I assume he'll proceed." I explained about Wren and the attempt on my life. "If that doesn't slow him down, nothing will."

"He needs to take the crown to solidify his rule, or the people will fight him," the king said. Looking at me, he nodded slowly. "Challenging him during the coronation could work."

"I imagine we can sneak onto the grounds during the

rush," Erleene said. "Everyone will want to be there. The roads will be packed with those arriving, and the castle itself and the grounds will be overrun with people setting up for the celebration."

"Hmm," Follen said. "How will we get the king to the front where others can see him?"

"I will take him through the inner realm," Erleene said. "I can deliver him at exactly the right time."

That was something we should've considered with the ball.

"The rest of us can wait in the audience, ready to support the rightful king and sway the crowd," Elion said.

"I can't think of anything else we could do," the king said, looking around at us. "Can you?"

"Could you get to Aillun in some other way?" I asked. "Confront him in his quarters?

"His guards are loyal to him alone," Ivaran said. "I'm sure he cast spells to ensure this."

"He did," Elion said, describing how he'd tried to convince them, but that they remained convinced the true king was dead by Elion's hand.

"What's keeping Aillun from casting a spell on everyone attending the coronation?" I asked.

"No one is that powerful."

"Not even Maverna's son?" I asked. "We haven't talked about how we'll stop her from interfering."

"Leave her to me," Erleene said grimly. "She and I have something to settle, and now is the time."

Ivaran grunted. "Just keep her out of the way."

"I would be delighted to do so," Erleene said.

I worried this plan would fail like sneaking into the ball had, but other than storming the castle with soldiers we didn't have, there didn't appear to be any other options.

"We need to remain hidden until tomorrow," I said, leaning into Elion's side. We hadn't addressed his curse, and time ticked away. But the king had ideas for breaking it, and he must care as much as me about making sure it didn't play out. I had to trust that installing him back on the throne would give him the chance to ensure the curse was broken. That and whatever Erleene planned to do with Maverna.

"Kill her," I blurted out, remembering what Latarre had said.

Elion grinned down at me. "Who should we kill?"

"Latarre told me if we killed Maverna, your curse might be broken." I explained that Latarre was the griffin who helped me in the inner realm.

"You trust him?" Elion asked.

I nodded. "He's on our side. I promise."

"Very well," the king said. "We need as many allies as possible."

"As for believing killing Maverna will end the spell, that notion has never been proven, I'm afraid," Follen said. "Maverna is not easily killed. It would take a special kind of magic."

"We need to try," I said. Anything was worth the risk. I had to save Elion.

"I will do my best to see this done," Erleene said. "For you, niece, and for Elion."

"Thank you."

We went through the plan several times, working out any potential issues, hoping we weren't missing anything.

"So, we wait for morning," Follen said.

"Is there a safe place we can stay where Aillun and Maverna won't find us?" I asked.

"I will take the king somewhere through the inner realm," Erleene said. "We will meet here tomorrow morning and go through the plan again?"

We all nodded.

"I will hide in the forest," Follen said, peering in that direction. "I imagine I can sleep in a tree."

That left me and Elion.

"I will take you somewhere safe through the realm as well," he said, holding out his hand.

I took it and, in a wink, we walked along the clouds with mist floating around us. We said nothing, not wanting to draw attention to anything hunting nearby.

Another flash, and we stood in a meadow high in the mountains with tiny flowers blooming all around us.

Elion waved his hand, and a large tent appeared along the edge of the open area.

"It's safe here?" I asked.

He smiled. "This is the outer edge of the kingdom. No one will come near here tonight, love. To make sure, I will use a protection spell."

My spine loosened, and we entered the tent that contained a big bed covered with sumptuous bedding, a trunk that might hold clothing, a steaming tub of water big enough for two, plus a table holding a tray loaded with food.

"Perfect," I said, turning and pressing myself against him. Heat flared through me, as it always did when he was near, and I knew I'd feel this way about him even if I reached one hundred.

He stroked the hair from my face and ran the back of his knuckles down my cheek. His kiss followed, and his fingers trailed fire along my sides.

We helped each other out of our clothing, and he picked me up and carried me to the tub, setting me gently inside before joining me and tugging me onto his lap.

"We have tonight," I said, my heart full of love. I turned to face him, to wrap my legs and arms around him, savoring his heat.

His mouth hovered over mine. "And we must not waste a second."

Chapter 38
Elion

As discussed, we met up in the meadow. After agreeing this was the best plan, we slowly made our way to the main road leading to the castle. It was crowded with what looked like every fae person in the kingdom. The regular people making up the backbone of my nation outnumbered royals many times over. They may not possess much magic, but they had a power of their own—that of their numbers.

This was a good plan. The ball interruption may have worked, but Aillun would not be able to control everyone attending the coronation in the way he could a smaller amount in the ballroom.

And King Khaidill had been well-loved. People would rejoice to see him alive.

Aillun had never been a favorite among those living throughout the kingdom.

Rather than don magical disguises Aillun could detect, we'd chosen instead to dress like the commoners.

The king guided the beasts pulling the wagon where the rest of us rode, all of us wearing simple clothing, the males with hats stuffed low on our heads, plus long beards affixed to our faces that Erleene had obtained from a shop far from the castle.

Was this enough disguise to get us close to the elevated platform where Aillun would be crowned? It had to be.

The king steered the beasts in among the others streaming toward the castle. We passed guards who studied those on the road, but their gazes skimmed right over us. It made me wonder if Erleene had somehow cloaked us with a light yet undetectable magic.

As if she heard my thought, she nodded. She and Follen sat on bales of hay opposite Raven and I. We stretched our legs out while we leaned against the rough wooden boards supporting the sides.

When we spied a line of guards blocking off the road ahead, the king turned the cart onto a big open field. Others had the same good idea, staking their beasts to trees and the ground. They'd left feed and water for them, then continued on foot.

Without speaking, we did the same, splitting up as we drew closer to the guards, mingling with the enormous crowd pushing their way toward the enormous building looming ahead.

Earlier, Erleene had used the inner realm to spy and discovered the coronation would take place on the back lawn. They'd erected a huge platform and mounted a gilded throne where Aillun would sit while he presided over the celebration that would follow him being crowned king.

The guards studied each person who passed, but none called out or paid us any attention, which could be due to the huge volume of fae making their way toward the castle.

We'd nearly been caught enacting our prior plan, but Aillun would have no idea about our intentions. He must feel confident by now that he'd gain the crown and that he'd be able to hold it.

I squeezed Raven's hand. With only a week left before my curse ran out, I only wanted to spend time with her. Hopefully we'd settle things with the true king —my father—today, and Raven and I could go somewhere together if the curse could not be broken.

I didn't hold out any hope of ending it. We hadn't heard from Nuvian, though he'd have a hard time reaching out. If he'd discovered anything, he would've found a way to tell me.

I didn't want Raven sacrificing anything to save me.

We made our way around the castle, pausing to take in the work that had been done to get ready for this big event. Brightly colored flags flickered in the breeze from poles marching around the back lawn area. In the shade of the castle, they'd set up the platform where Aillun would be crowned. The base appeared about twice my height.

I was pleased to note stairs on both sides leading to the top. Guards stood at the base of each to keep the crowd from encroaching, but we'd expected that. Erleene would go with the king and disarm them.

People gathered at the base, spreading out on the enormous lawn area. Some stood, but most had taken seats and set up picnics to enjoy while they waited, turning this into a full-day event.

Aillun and Maverna had not yet made an appearance, but I assumed they'd arrive just prior to the ceremony. Maverna wouldn't miss the chance to beam while the plan she started before I was born was finally fulfilled.

Anger burned through me. She'd murdered my mother and stolen my life from me. For that and for everything she'd done since, she must pay.

We got as close to the platform as we dared.

The murmur of the crowd nearly deafened me as we sat on the ground, holding hands. By now, Erleene, Follen, and the king would've made their way close to one set of stairs. They'd act the moment Aillun appeared on the platform, stepping down the ramp projecting off the balcony from the second floor of the castle.

Raven leaned into my side, and I put my arm around her, savoring this moment together. The sun shone down, generating just enough heat so we were comfortable, but not enough to make us hot. Her cheeks had pinkened, and I adjusted her straw hat to cover her face.

"Love you," she said softly.

My heart overflowed with affection for her. "No matter what happens, I'm grateful we've had this time together."

She rubbed my thigh. "Don't say that. It's not over yet."

It wasn't, but I couldn't see a way beyond the curse's natural end. Would my final moment hurt, or would I just slip from this world and into whatever came next? No one knew what happened when we died. Humans believed in a place called heaven. Maybe I'd go there. I would wait for Raven, then be there with a smile on my face when she one day arrived.

A commotion above drew everyone's eyes, and cheers rang out from the crowd as Aillun strode down the ramp from the balcony, taking his spot in front of the throne. He waved with both arms, and the crowd roared, rising to their feet to greet him.

Maverna slunk down the ramp and stood beside him, as did another woman, who wore a large hat that shadowed her face.

I frowned, though I wasn't sure where my confusion came from.

But . . . I knew her.

It was Axilya, the fae who'd guided the human women throughout the events of the bride matching program.

She shifted to the side, and I sensed she didn't feel comfortable being on display. I wasn't sure why Aillun needed her there. They weren't related as far as I knew, and she was a relatively minor member of the fae aristocracy.

I'd started to dismiss her when her gaze swept across

the crowd. It landed on me, and a mix of fear and rage flashed in her eyes.

It suddenly hit me. I'd seen her somewhere other than during the bride events, but where?

Oh...

The memory crashed down on me, the one I'd been spelled to forget.

She was the one who'd had an affair with the man I'd called father.

She'd murdered him, and then she'd made me forget.

Chapter 39
Raven

Elion leaped to his feet and pointed to the stand. "Murderer!"

"What?" I said, tugging on his sleeve, worried about him drawing attention.

People turned to stare, some shaking their heads.

"Before my eyes, Axilya murdered the man I called father. She cast a spell on me to forget, and only now do I remember." He pointed again and raised his voice. "Murderer!"

The crowd erupted, some backing away from us, others glaring.

We hadn't spoken of providing a distraction. As far as I knew, we were here to lead the crowd in support of King Khaidill when he appeared on the platform.

"You murdered my father," Elion shouted in dismay. "You had an affair with him, and then you killed him because he didn't want you."

In the uproar, no one but me noticed Ivaran, Erleene,

and Follen slipping past the guards and climbing the stairs. Even Aillun didn't see them until King Khaidill had reached the top of the platform.

"Arrest him," King Khaidill cried out, pointing at Aillun. "He tried to murder me and steal the crown!"

The crowd went wild, many calling out Ivaran's name, others weeping in joy.

Maverna lifted her arms and lightning shot down from the sky, hitting the platform and showering the crowd with sparks.

Silence descended. Many shuffled their feet, while others ran, bolting toward the woods.

"How dare you?" Maverna bellowed, stepping between Aillun, who looked ready to run himself, and the true king.

"No," Erleene said, striding toward Maverna. "How dare you? You murdered Queen Lensa while she was recovering after giving birth to the real prince."

"Real prince?" People cried out. Only a few stomped their feet and shouted that Aillun was the real prince.

"Elion is the true prince," Erleene shouted above the calls. "Maverna killed Queen Lensa and switched infants, depositing Elion with the fae who raised him as his parents. Arrest her!" Her magic snapped out, hitting Maverna, who reeled backward.

Maverna wasn't going to go down easily, however. Shooting magic back at Erleene, she shrieked.

I cupped the blue stone Latarre gave me and released a heartfelt whisper. *I need you. Please help.*

Latarre stepped out onto the balcony behind them.

With a heavy growl, he bound Maverna with magical spells. She wailed and shook, and though I could tell she was trying to leap into the inner realm, the bindings must prevent her from escaping.

King Khaidill descended on Aillun with guards, who quickly subdued him and started hauling him toward the balcony. I wasn't sure what the king would do with Aillun, but the attempted murder of the man you called father should come with a stiff penalty.

Elion raced toward the stairs, and I followed. I had my own agenda as far as Maverna was concerned.

We bolted up the stairs, arriving on the platform as the king stood before the crowd, his arms lifted to receive their cries of happiness.

Erleene and Follen battled magically with Axilya, who for some reason, glared at me before fighting them off. They collapsed on the platform, unconscious.

Elion and I raced toward Axilya.

"You must die," she cried, and at first, I thought she meant Elion. Then I realized she was looking right at me.

It suddenly clicked. *She* was the one who'd killed my friends. I didn't know why, but she'd done it.

She shot a bolt of magic at Elion. He cried out and fell onto the platform.

"No!" I raced around him, determined to protect him with my life. I'd sacrifice myself rather than let her harm him further.

As I expected, she turned her magic on me. Her spell flew my way, and I braced myself for a killing blow.

"Love you, Elion," I whispered.

Before her bolt could hit me, someone leaped between us, taking what was meant for me.

Latarre crumpled onto the platform in front of me, gazing up at me with so much emotion in his eyes, it cut through me.

"I'm sorry, daughter," he said, his eyes shadowing, and his voice only a harsh murmur. "I tried to . . . save you."

Chapter 40
Elion

I woke to find Raven standing over me, her eyes closed, and her arms lifted to fire magic.

"I love you, Elion," she murmured. "Always."

Power shot out from her fingers, hitting Axilya. A pop, and the other woman turned to dust that drifted down to land on the platform.

Raven turned her attention on Maverna. "You." As I struggled to rise, I gaped in horror at a partly shifted griffen—Latarre—plus Erleene and Follen lying nearby. My father lay on the platform, his arms pinned behind his back and his ankles secured together.

Maverna smirked as Raven rushed toward her.

"What do you think you can do, puny human?" Maverna asked. Her hand swept toward Aillun, releasing his magical ties.

He grinned and rose to his feet. "Thanks, Mother." He strode over to stand at the front of the platform. "Pay no attention to these imposters," he cried out to the crowd. "They are cloaked with magic to appear like our poor murdered King Khaidill, and a few mistaken followers of this fiend."

"The one who put this together is still in his true form." Maverna glared at me. "Elion. I believe it is time for your curse to run out, don't you?"

But before she could sweep her deadly magic my way, Raven leaped, releasing a hoarse cry. She hit Maverna hard, and the two women fell to the platform and rolled across the surface. They came to rest with Raven straddling Maverna.

"No more. No more," Raven bellowed. Her hand plunged down, hitting Maverna's chest hard. Magic shot out from the impact, but Raven didn't stop there. She pressed harder, ignoring Maverna's screams and flailing arms.

With a hoarse cry, Aillun ran to them and tried to pull Raven off his mother.

I hauled Aillun up with magic and tossed him aside. He hit the wall of the castle and slumped onto the balcony. Confused guards crowded around him, looking from him to me, indecision clear on their faces.

Did they finally realize the king lived?

Raven growled and pushed harder, shoving into Maverna's chest. The other woman gulped and smacked Raven, but her blows weakened. Her hands flopped on the platform as Raven ripped her hand out of Maverna's chest.

"This, you evil bitch," Raven yelled, "I do with my

heartmagic. Erleene was right. They said I could do this and I am. You should never have touched Elion!"

She rose to shaky feet and lifted her hand with Maverna's heart over her head.

"More heartmagic coming right up." Her eyes pinched closed, and wind whipped around us as she gathered magic.

She shot it at the heart, and it burst into flame, smoking and shooting sparks until nothing remained.

Raven's arms dropped to her sides. For a moment, I worried she'd fall. I struggled to rise, determined to go to her, but could only get to my knees.

Leaving Maverna's corpse, Raven staggered over to me. She dropped to the platform in front of me, and her arms wrapped around me.

"It's over," she whispered. "I hope it's over."

I held her while she sobbed.

It wasn't long before she tugged away. "I have to go to . . . my father." Her gaze, so full of pain and sorrow, met mine. "Latarre is my father! All this time . . ." She shook her head, and her voice dropped to almost nothing. "All this time, he was my father."

She rushed over to Latarre and dropped to her knees beside him. He'd shifted completely to his fae form.

While I released my father from Maverna's magical bindings and helped him to his feet, Raven stroked Latarre's forehead. Tears streamed down her face, and it gutted me to see them.

I wanted to go to her, but I had to make sure this was truly over.

Axilya had disintegrated. All this time, she'd been killing the human women to cover her attempts on Raven's life. By loving my wife, I'd endangered her.

The curse she'd laid on the man who raised me ran through my mind.

"You have wronged me. Scorned me."

She'd cast the spell that would haunt every generation born after him forever. Except I wasn't his son by blood, so the spell hadn't fallen on me. She'd been determined to make sure I wasn't happy with anyone.

"No one in your family will love. This I swear. You and yours are doomed!"

When I hadn't succumbed, she must've started to worry I'd remember her murdering the man I believed was my father. She'd come after me, and then Raven.

Her hatred had known no boundaries. Raven and I had almost paid the ultimate price.

"Arrest him and place him in the dungeon under heavy wards," my father shouted, pointing at Aillun. "He is charged with attempted murder!"

The crowd roared, many crying out King Khaidill's name, some even weeping.

All the energy had left the fae man who'd been so desperate to be king. He'd seen Raven destroy Maverna. He must fear he would be next.

He held out his hands for the guards to bind him, and with a flash, they disappeared, taking him to the cells deep below the castle. It would be ironic if they placed him in mine.

The true king strode to the edge of the platform and explained to the audience what they'd just witnessed.

I rose and went to Raven, holding her while she cried for her father. If only there was something I could do to ease her pain.

I should've guessed who he was; there was something about him I'd found familiar, though I had never seen him before in my life.

"I got my claws from him," she said, lifting her hands that contained only smooth nails. "He's part griffin shifter, though I didn't inherit his glorious wings or his ability to shift."

"You're amazing no matter what blood runs through your veins," I said.

"Is there anything we can do for him?" she lamented, her palm resting on Latarre's chest. "I don't know if he's dead or alive or somehow suspended." She turned tear-filled eyes my way. "The thought of losing him when I've just found him . . . It's horrible, Elion. Horrible."

Latarre groaned, and his eyes opened. He looked up at Raven with so much love it made my breath catch.

"Daughter," he whispered, then stronger. "My beloved daughter, Raven. You look so much like your mother. My Rosalie. If only . . ."

"We need healers," my father cried out, glancing our way. "Healers!"

Multiple fae appeared beside the king and bowed. He waved to Latarre, and they rushed over to assess him. In seconds, they'd disappeared, taking him to where they could help him recover.

"Will he be okay?" Raven asked, shuddering in my arms.

"I believe he will. Our healers are amazing. And he was awake, speaking. That's a good sign."

She released a sigh full of relief and pain and nestled in my arms. "I love you, Elion."

"I love you, little human."

I didn't know why her father left her mother and returned to the fae kingdom, but I suspected we'd find out one day.

But I was grateful my love would be given the chance to know him better.

Chapter 41
Raven

Maverna was dead by my own hand and power, but we didn't know if this broke Elion's curse. It wasn't something that could be seen or felt by anyone in the kingdom.

He showed me the scroll that suggested a sacrifice could end it. I'd been willing to die to save him. Had that been enough?

My love could be dead within a week, and the thought was ripping me apart.

After the announcement that the king was alive and that Aillun had tried to kill him, the crowd went wild, cheering for King Khaidill. Many called for Aillun's head. Aillun now resided in the dungeon, though he was completely subdued after watching me rip his mother's heart from her chest and incinerate it with magic.

I still wasn't sure how I'd done it. When she threatened Elion, rage poured through me, fueling something deep inside me. I'd stood over him and called on magic I hadn't realized I possessed.

They found Camile lurking inside the castle, and the king's guards caught her. My father-in-law banished her from the kingdom, and I hoped I'd never see her again.

Instead of Aillun's coronation, the kingdom held a party to celebrate that the true king still lived. It went on for days, and by the time everyone left, we were exhausted.

Erleene and Follen remained behind, sliding into new roles as advisors to the king, though Erleene first went to retrieve Koko, bringing him directly to me.

My little pet appeared miffed that I'd left him behind, but he soon got over his snit and savored playing with his siblings again. Thankfully, Aillun hadn't harmed the king's reshas.

Aillun was tried, convicted, and banished to the inner realm with an unbreakable spell that prevented him from ever leaving. No one spoke of him after that. He'd tried to kill his father, and now he would pay the ultimate price.

As for Nuvian and Betts, they'd opted to remain at Elion's estate that was no longer encased in ice. The woman Elion had called his sister said she didn't want it. She'd fled the kingdom once she heard the news, and good riddance. She'd sounded like a complete jerk. How dare she reject Elion because he was cursed and scarred?

Latarre slowly recovered, and I visited him each day. We didn't speak about anything personal, just rejoiced that he lived.

Two days before the end of Elion's curse, Latarre and I took a long walk together through the castle grounds. Koko scampered with us, stopping to sniff every flower along the way. My fox-kitty was growing. Soon, he'd be as big as his parents.

"You're half-griffin?" I asked Latarre.

"Yes, which means you're one-quarter griffin." He stared toward the woods, and I wondered if he ached to run there, to give into that side of himself he'd kept hidden while staying in the castle.

"I can only manifest claws." I held up my hands, showing my smooth nails. Unless I worked hard at it, my claws didn't appear, but I doubted I'd need them now that my enemies had been vanquished.

"I'm surprised they appear for you at all," he said. "It's rare for one with so little shifter blood to do even that."

We continued around the side of the castle, him pointing out various flowers, me trying to find a way to ask the biggest question lurking in my mind. Finally, I spit it out.

"Why did you leave me and Mom?" I asked. The question had hovered on the tip of my tongue from the moment I'd discovered who he was.

I should be grateful he lived, right? I was, but the hurt I'd felt since Mom told me about my dad was burning a hole in my belly.

"Maverna discovered I had a child. Foretelling spells suggested you could bring about her death." His intent gaze met mine, and we stopped on the crushed stone path with the scent of tessilar lilies floating around us. "From that moment, she hunted you. I couldn't endanger your life by remaining with your mother because I'd lead her to you." The sadness in his eyes made my throat tighten. "I loved your mother so much."

"Mom died."

His face tightened with grief. "She meant everything to me. I cast a protective spell over you both, but I couldn't deepen it. I've spent years luring Maverna. Each time she'd get close, believing when she caught me, she'd find you, I would move again. I could only remain hidden in the inner realm. But it was too dangerous to bring you or your mother there." He stopped and held my shoulders, and the intensity of his voice sunk into me like a soothing balm, dispelling some of my anger and sadness. "When I saw you in that cave, I knew who you were. You have your mother's eyes."

They stung with the tears I'd held back throughout my life. I'd refused to cry for someone who rejected me.

But now they fell, for my mom, for him, and for myself. We'd all missed out on so much.

"I hope in time, you'll find a way to forgive me," he said.

Unable to cling to anger, I hugged him, and there wasn't anything better than when my dad hugged me back.

Koko sat at our feet, watching us. He yipped when he saw us hugging, and I stooped down and stroked his little face.

We finished our walk, and my footsteps felt lighter.

By the time we returned to the castle, I felt like something monumental had changed.

I knew me and my dad were going to be okay. We'd get to know each other better, and we'd have each other moving forward.

As the days drew to a close, I couldn't hold back my stress. His curse would claim him soon. I couldn't trust that killing Maverna had ended it.

King Khaidill called us into his private chamber when there were only two days left.

"I have not been able to locate anyone who can give me a straight answer," he said, slamming his fist on the arm of his chair. "A few witches say that when Raven killed Maverna, the curse ended. Others are less sure." Grief filled his eyes. "If only I could give you the answer you seek, son."

Elion dipped his head forward. He hadn't quite gotten to the point where he was willing to name the king as his father to his face, but he was close. Knowing he might die had made him re-evaluate everything in his life.

He loved me; that was a given. He'd respected the king for a very long time. It wasn't hard for the love he'd had for his liege lord to change into the love of a parent. If he lived, I had a feeling he and King Khaidill would grow closer.

"Thank you for trying," Elion said, squeezing my hand.

"Yes."

"I won't give up," he cried in desperation, climbing

off the dais and hugging Elion. "I will never give up, my son."

On what could be our last day together, we took a walk far from the castle. Coming across a pretty meadow, we spread out a blanket and dropped the basket of food we'd brought with us, settling beside it.

"Love me," he said softly, cupping my face.

"I always will." I struggled not to cry, not wanting to spend what could be our last few hours together wallowing in tears.

I tugged at his clothing while he did the same with mine, then we fell onto the blanket.

He rose over me, his gaze never leaving mine. "I will watch out for you no matter where I am. Know this."

"Elion," I gulped out. "It can't be over."

"Not yet," he said, his mouth claiming mine. His touch seared through me, each stroke of his fingers delivering pure heaven.

As he claimed me fully, our gazes remained locked. He moved within me. Our bodies were so in tune that we came at the same time.

After, he held me. We didn't bother to eat because that would mean moving away from each other.

If I clung to him, would I be able to keep the curse from taking him?

Eventually, the sun began to set. We returned to the castle, entering through a back entrance, and hurried up the stairs to our room.

There, we lay on our bed together.

I couldn't stop shivering. He bundled us up in blankets and sat in a chair, holding me, clinging as I did with him.

Time ticked away, and midnight approached.

When the big old clock in the foyer began chiming twelve, I turned in his lap and wrapped myself around him.

"Love you, Raven," he whispered at eight strikes. He kissed the woven matebond symbol on my wrist.

"So much," he said at ten. "Knowing you feel the same is all that matters."

"I do. Always, love." Always.

"Bae mae frael liethrà, an ular fieair al laitlen ru mae sleedest," he whispered as the eleventh and twelfth chimes echoed up the stairwell. These were the words he'd said when we married.

I kept my gaze on his, waiting, everything inside me clenched tight. I couldn't bear it if I lost him, but—

The twelfth gong ended, leaving us alone in silence.

He pinched his eyes closed and opened them again.

I didn't dare breathe.

"You're still with me," I whispered, clinging to his shoulders. Tears fell down my face unchecked.

His heart beat strongly beneath my palm when I stroked his chest.

"It's over. I'm with you, Raven." The beginning of a smile shone on his face. He took my hand and kissed it. "Forever, love."

I rose and kissed him, whispering against his lips. "Forever."

Chapter 42
Epilogue

Elion

One year later

I paced the outer room of the large suite within the castle that I shared with Raven. For hours, I'd remained near her, my body consumed with stress. But my anxiety was nothing compared to the suffering Raven was going through now.

Raven's father stood at the bank of windows, peering out, more sedate than I could ever imagine being. He kept commenting about the trees, birds, and even flowers. How could I think of anything like that right now?

The door opened, and we looked in that direction.

"Is the baby here yet?" Raven's younger sister, Emme, bounced into the room, followed by Maecia, the elf woman who'd cared for Raven after she arrived. We'd hired her to entertain and educate Emme when she visited the fae realm and we weren't available to do so ourselves. "Am I an auntie yet?"

"Not yet. Soon, I hope." I stooped down and held out my arms, and she scooted to me so fast, she almost knocked me over. I gave her a long hug. This child brought so much joy to our lives.

"I want to take the baby for walks and she can come to my tea parties." Many of which she'd held since she arrived here to visit the first time. We shared raising her with Raven's cousin, who loved the little girl as much as me and Raven. This way, Emme experienced the best of both worlds.

"She, huh?" I asked with a smile, straightening. "What makes you think it's a girl?"

She shrugged. "I just know."

"Come along now," Maecia said. She gave me a nod and escorted Emme from the room.

I resumed pacing. "What is taking so long?"

My father strolled into the room and sat in a big chair, watching me for a long while, his fingers tapping on the chair arm. "You know that striding about will not make this happen any sooner, son." Despite the dryness in his voice, his eyes sparkled with excitement. This was a momentous event for the kingdom.

I stopped moving and glared at him, my hands on my hips. "How can you be relaxed at a time like this?"

Raven's muffled cry rang out. It chilled down my spine and made my heart burn.

Even her father, sitting quietly in a chair nearby, started to look concerned.

"Enough," I said, striding toward the door. "I will not remain here any longer."

My father leapt up and somehow got ahead of me. He braced his palms on the doorframe to hold me back with his body.

"You cannot go in there," he said. "It's not done."

"I don't care," I said as another cry reached me. "Don't you see? I can't leave her alone at a time like this." I lowered my voice. "Please, step aside, father."

As with each time I called him that, he grinned.

"Since you asked so nicely, son, I will do this for you. Perhaps, if I'd been with your mother when you were born, things might've been different. It's just that . . . the witches don't want us to be present."

"She needs me, and that's all that matters."

"Your love is known throughout the kingdom."

How could anyone see anything less? We'd been inseparable since it was clear my curse was over and I'd lived. All I wanted was to be with my wife, my love, my Raven.

"And because you love her so," my father said, "I understand. No one should stand in your way." He moved aside, and I opened the door. "As king, I will do away with the rule that only witches are allowed to be present at the birth of a future king."

"You cannot be here," one of the three witches cried

out as I stepped inside. "I do not care what a puny king says. It is forbidden."

I shifted her aside, though gently. "Raven needs me."

"Elion," she called out, her hand lifting.

I crossed the room quickly and shifted Koko to the side so I could sit beside Raven on the bed. Sweat coated her pink face, and I'd never seen anyone more beautiful in my life.

Koko whimpered, staring up at me as if he thought I could fix this. I wished I could.

Raven's gaze met mine. "It hurts." When her belly began to clench, she gasped.

"Push," one of the witches said, glaring at me, but wisely choosing to say nothing further about my presence.

"It is nearly time for this young fae prince or princess to be born," the other witch said.

I climbed all the way onto the bed, moving until I was behind Raven, holding her with my legs spread around her.

She pushed and strained, her groans echoing in the room.

And when she cried out one last time, our daughter joined us in the world.

Raven looked up at me with so much joy on her face, I couldn't breathe. "She's gorgeous. I think she has your eyes."

"She is incredibly lovely. So are you." I kissed her while the witches cooed and bathed our daughter.

And when they laid her in Raven's arms, she leaned

over to kiss our daughter's cheek. "Welcome, Rosalie Lensa. We will love you forever."

Latarre stood in the open doorway. "Named for your mother, Raven?" He choked up, wiping his eyes. "My Rosalie. I miss her so much."

"Come see her—your new granddaughter," I said, overcome with emotion. I couldn't love Raven or my little girl any more than I did at this moment.

Latarre approached the bed cautiously. "You are well, daughter?"

She smiled. "Much better now." Her gaze, so full of emotion, met mine before returning to our child. "Would you look at her? She's amazing."

"As are you, Raven," my father said, joining us. "My Lensa." He peered upward. "Do you see this, love? A new Lensa has been born. A new beginning for our people." He stepped closer, his eyes bright with tears. "I thank you for this precious gift."

Raven smiled, nodding before her loving gaze fell on me. "She's us, Elion. You and me and our worlds combined."

As my father and Raven's left to spread the good news throughout the kingdom, I leaned over Raven and kissed her. Then I kissed my daughter's forehead. My heart split wide open but refilled just by gazing into Raven's eyes.

There was nothing better than the life we'd built together.

Ava Ross

~THE END~

I hope you've enjoyed Elion & Raven's story!
Sigh. I'm going to miss these characters and this world.
Would you mind leaving a review?
THANKS!

Have you read any of my sci-fi romance?
Now you can. I've included Chapter 1 of
Nailing the Alien here.
Just turn the page . . .

About the Author

Ava Ross is a two-time *USA Today* Bestselling author who has written numerous titles. She fell for men with unusual features when she first watched Star Wars, where alien creatures have gone mainstream. She lives in New England with her husband (who is sadly not an alien, though he is still cute in his own way), her kids, and a few assorted pets.

Series by AVA

Mail-Order Brides of Crakair

Brides of Driegon

Fated Mates of the Ferlaern Warriors

Fated Mates of the Xilan Warriors

Holiday with a Cu'zod Warrior

Galaxy Games

*Alien Warrior Abandoned/
Shattered Galaxies*

Beastly Alien Boss

Bride of the Fae

Ava Ross

Screamer Woods
Orc Me Baby One More Time

Stranded With an Alien
Frost

You can find my books on Amazon.

NAILING THE ALIEN

My short-term construction job with a grumpy orc boss just got complicated.

Desperate to escape the clutches of the alien lizard mafia, I accept a spur-of-the-moment job offer on a distant planet. A monstrous, grumpy alien orc is building a new home in a distant colony, and he's looking for an assistant.

He needs me to hold his hammer. I get it. It's a big hammer.

He's a lonely barbarian brute with a gruff exterior, but I soon learn that inside he's hiding a squishy center. When he unexpectedly enters his mating frenzy, there's no one around to handle the job . . . except me. He gives me two options—return home or stay and help him with a whole different kind of nailing . . .

Nailing the Alien is Book 1 in the Beastly Alien Boss Series. Each features a rough and ready alien who can't resist falling for his fated mate.

Chapter 1
CORA

I raced through the street with three Vessars snapping at my heels. My sneakers slammed on the cracked concrete, and I barely avoided placing my foot in something dead, flat, and slimy.

This was my damn cousin's fault. If he were around, I'd load him in a rocket launcher and shoot him all the way to the Dundire Quadrant.

He bailed from Earth three days ago, taking a one-way shuttle to who knows where, leaving me to clean up his mess. His mess being a sizeable debt owed to the Vessar alien lizard mafia.

They seemed to think they could collect it from me. Haha. I didn't even have enough credits to buy a cup of juva. And if I showed up on my mom's stoop to beg, she'd slam the door in my face. We got along best when we didn't talk or see each other.

As for my dad, I wasn't sure who he was, and Mom wasn't telling.

The Vessars growled, their breath hot on the back of my neck.

"No problem," the Vessar boss had said. "You can paysss hisss debt wit youself. I sellsss to someone decent. Promise."

Like I believed his promise?

No can do, dudes. I liked my simple life, and I planned to keep it auction-free. A sale meant slavery to an alien for the rest of my days.

A Vessar's suction-cupped limb snapped out, hitting my right shoulder hard enough that I staggered. I didn't fall, though. I *couldn't* fall. If I did, they'd catch me. Drag me back to the mafia boss.

I'd never be seen again.

Mom wouldn't miss me. My cousin wouldn't know or care. Only a few friends might ask where I was and why I up and left without selling my one-room apartment.

Breaking free of the Vessar, I wrenched forward. I ran faster, fleeing around the corner with enormous city buildings looming around me. Shuttles zipped overhead, low enough that the breeze from their passage made my long hair whip my face. I shoved it aside as I bolted onto the main thoroughfare, shoving people and various aliens aside.

My pace slowed when I reached the lifted sidewalk. I shot a glance over my shoulder. The Vessars followed, their three eyes keeping me in sight. They ignored the goods on display in shops lining the right side of the walk.

If I were lucky, I'd lose them in the open market

ahead. They could be relentless, but I had patience and determination. I'd outlast them.

A Vessar came up close behind me, his low hissing voice raking down my spine. "Come wit usssss. We be kind."

Like I'd believe something like that? There was nothing kind about being sold.

"I'm a free citizen," I said, hoping the creature didn't hear the shake in my voice. "This is Jake's problem. You have no right to come after me."

"Gives creditssss for cousin, and we leavessss."

I could drain my account and sign over my next few year's earnings, but what would I use to live on after that? With only a rudimentary education, I couldn't secure a high-paying job. Ten years after moving out of Mom's house at eighteen, and I still wasn't much better off.

"Leave me alone," I said, keeping my voice soft. While some might rush to my defense if I screamed, others would crowd around and cheer while the Vessar mafia minions pinned me down and tied me up.

A suckered limb coiled around my arm. Bold of him, but no one was looking this way.

After prying the suction cups off my arm, I broke into a jog, darting around couples strolling and families pausing to gape through shop windows.

A sign ahead, Intergalactic Employment Agency, drew my eye. I wasn't looking for a job, but I could hide inside until the Vessars gave up and slunk away.

Maybe it was time I sold my apartment and moved to

a distant colony. If I took care with my trail, the Vessars wouldn't be able to follow.

When I stepped inside the Agency, a monotone chime rang out overhead. A flat, disc-like hover computer zipped from the back room and hovered close to my face.

"Recognition proceeding," it said.

I struggled not to cringe. It would record that I'd been here and—

Tiny lights flashed behind its dark view screen. "Cora Marie Westmore has been entered into the database. I am now sorting for available positions that fit your experience."

"Thank you, um . . . I'm not sure I'm truly looking for a job, but I'm open to exploring possibilities." That sounded neutral enough.

I nudged the droid to the side and glanced through the clear plexi behind me. The Vessars were fuming on the walk, their dusky blue cheeks darkening. They flailed their limbs, smacking those who passed by. I doubted they'd dare enter the building, since they'd been forbidden to interfere in matters of general commerce.

They didn't leave as I'd hoped, however. One leaned against a metal post on the opposite side of the walk, and the other two smooshed their faces against the plexi, keeping me in sight.

Did this place have a back door I could escape through?

"Do you have live personnel working today?" I asked. Anything to delay this process. If I remained here for hours, the Vessars might give up.

"I can page someone," the droid said. "However, I am well programmed and delighted to share job options with you. I note in your bio that you have considerable construction experience."

If you could count the carpenter's assistant job that I'd done for four years in my early twenties. The job was on Stellar 4, and despite the filter dome overhead, I'd gotten sunburned. As a bonus, I'd also gained ripped muscles, though I wasn't sure they'd hung around for long after I quit.

"Yes," I said when lights flashed behind the droid's view screen. It continued to hover in front of my face. "I do have construction experience. I've done all kinds of jobs, actually."

"Delightful. We have five positions open within this quadrant that suit your skills."

"What about," another look outside showed the damn Vessars still waiting. A growl ripped through me. How long would it take for them to give up?

"Two of these positions ask that the applicant arrive immediately," the droid continued. "A shuttle will transport you directly from here."

I frowned. "Like, *here*, here?"

"That is correct."

"What about my apartment?" I'd worked hard to buy it. I wouldn't abandon it to whoever chose to claim it.

"It would be secured until you returned."

"And my current job?"

"We have applicants waiting for this type of position."

It only paid a few credits more than minimum wage, but times were tough. No one was irreplaceable.

If I accepted a position off world, I'd escape the Vessars. I could arrange for my property to be sold and the credits deposited in my account. I wouldn't have to return to this city, and if I was lucky, the Vessars wouldn't discover where I'd gone.

The Vessars couldn't threaten a droid to give up this kind of information.

My mood perked up.

"Tell me more about the openings," I said.

"The first is in the Tricar Quadrant and involves—"

"Nope."

"Excuse me?" It whirled backward, huffing with pretend dismay.

Really, these droids were too lifelike. Creepy even. That's what the government wanted: friendly computers to make life pleasant for us citizens.

"The Tricar Quadrant is an icy wasteland," I said.

"The position pays well."

And we all knew why. "Tell me about the second position."

"A construction assistant position with a colony manager on planet Merth 4X7, helping build their residence."

A house on a distant colony, then. "I don't think I've heard of Merth . . ."

"4X7 is located in the Sebula Quadrant. A different individual had been hired for this position, but they abruptly backed out before the task could be concluded." The droid grumbled, though they didn't have true feelings. They were just programmed to act like they did.

It launched into a spiel to sell the job. "Merth 4X7 is an agricultural planet with three colonies, primarily growing hemp. Indigenous populations, none. Settlers, three thousand twenty-two, though few reside in the colony with this position. Water, potable. Air, breathable. Gravity is approximate to this planet. As far as the employer, the last to hold this position reported he—"

"The job sounds perfect," I jumped in to say as Vessar claws scraped down the plexi behind me. Would they be that daring?

With only the droid present, they might. I doubted a machine working at an employment agency was programmed to provide defense. The government wouldn't expect them to need something like that.

Nope, the droid would either watch while the Vessars took me, and then say nothing, or protest only to be reprogrammed by the lizard mafia to forget what happened.

"I'll take the second position," I said. "Transport me now."

"Of course," the droid said. A thin panel projected from beneath its viewing screen. "Please sign here."

I scrawled my name.

A hum erupted in the back of the small room, and a transport pod thumped down against the floor, coming to a stop. The hatch peeled open across the front.

"You will be transported in suspension, as Merth 4X7 is twenty-seven-point-two light years from Earth," the droid said.

Lovely. I'd only traveled in suspension a few times, and I'd been dizzy when I woke up. Still, this job would get me off Earth and away from the Vessar lizard mafia, hopefully forever.

"What's my boss's name?" I asked.

The droid paused, then spit it out. "Kreelevar Nohmal Trirag Grikohr."

"Say that one fast."

"Excuse me?"

The Vessars jangled the front door handle.

"It doesn't matter." Panic lifted my voice. "Get me out of here. Now."

The door slammed opened, and the Vessars tumbled into the room, slipping on the tiles and falling to the floor in a scramble of tangled, suction cup limbs.

"Of course," the droid said, glancing at the Vessars. "I will be with you shortly once I've made arrangements for this human." It turned back to me. "Thank you for stopping by. We at the Intergalactic Employment Agency appreciate your enthusiasm."

"Yeah, that's it. I'm wicked excited." I rushed to the pod and jumped inside. The hatch closed, and straps looped across my body, then tightened. A pinch on my arm was followed by my head spinning.

The Vessars clawed across the room, their limbs reaching toward me.

"Haha. You lose," I shouted, though I doubted they'd hear through the plexi shuttle lid.

My laugh echoed around me as the pod shot up through the chute, leaving the Vessars and my cousin's debt behind.

Get Nailing the Alien!

Printed in Great Britain
by Amazon